THREE PROSE WORKS

ELSE LASKER-SCHÜLER

THREE PROSE WORKS

*Translated from the German and
with an afterword by James J. Conway*

RIXDORF EDITIONS BERLIN 2022

The Peter Hille Book by Else Lasker-Schüler was first published in German as *Das Peter Hille-Buch* by Axel Juncker Verlag in Stuttgart and Berlin, 1906. This translation is based on the slightly revised second edition published by Paul Cassirer in Berlin, 1919.

The Nights of Tino of Baghdad by Else Lasker-Schüler was first published in German as *Die Nächte Tino von Bagdads* by Axel Juncker Verlag in Berlin, Stuttgart and Leipzig, 1907. This translation is based on the revised second edition published as *Die Nächte der Tino von Bagdad* by Paul Cassirer in Berlin, 1919, and was originally issued by Rixdorf Editions in 2019 as a PDF (978-3-947325-05-4) to its mailing list.

The Prince of Thebes by Else Lasker-Schüler was first published in German as *Der Prinz von Theben* by Verlag der weißen Bücher in Leipzig, 1914. This translation is based on the slightly revised second edition published by Paul Cassirer in Berlin, 1920.

This anthology, translation and afterword © 2019–2022 James J. Conway

Three Prose Works
first published Rixdorf Editions, Berlin, 2022

Design by Svenja Prigge, cover image based on illustrations depicting figures from *One Thousand and One Nights* produced by the Dresdner Kunstanstalt, c. 1900

ISBN: 978-3-947325-12-2

All rights reserved. No part of this publication may be reproduced, stored in a retrieval system, or transmitted, in any form or by any means, without the prior written permission of Rixdorf Editions, except for legitimate review purposes.

RixdorfEditions.com

CONTENTS

THE PETER HILLE BOOK	7
THE NIGHTS OF TINO OF BAGHDAD	87
THE PRINCE OF THEBES	133
Afterword	183

THE PETER HILLE BOOK

weariness towards the morning bells, and blissful memories arose from Petrus's Palm Sunday eyes – reverently I stood on my toes to peer in. And as we stood before the church, he opened the heavy door. Mothers were praying to the Holy Mother while children laid flowers before the Child of Stars, and for the first time I saw men made of stone who looked like Petrus; they too had coarse hair and long beards and kept their heads bowed but none had a crest like his. And the Nazarene was waiting on the cross in eternal suffering, so firmly nailed, so blood-nailed, so forsaken … 'Take him off the cross, take him off the cross!' – And outside the earth prayed to the sun, and the youths were standing on the stairs waiting for us; they were fair, and even the plump fool resembled a comical grotesque from a rare pagan ornament in the imperial treasury.

PETRUS AND THE SHEPHERD

The sky filled with blue. The cool air was fragrant, it was May. Petrus and I were rowed across the little river, and once we were on the other side a young shepherd came towards us with his bleating charges. 'So the little black sheep that you carry on your back must be your favourite?' And the boy nodded ... 'It is mine, the other lambs are my master's.' 'He treats it as tenderly as a mother,' said Petrus, and for a long time after the kindly shepherd kept turning around to look for Knecht Ruprecht and his fierce beard. And for the first time I showed him my child. He was sitting on my shoulder like a little rider. Petrus had never seen him, but now, as he lifted him up high, he said: 'The eye of your child is a clear star,' and now he knew why I so often whispered and sang all sorts of things in the evening – tumble-bumble songs.

PETRUS'S BIRTHDAY

The following day ... was the day of Petrus, for he was born on that day. And in the morning his favourites came and brought him presents, and the other youths and maidens adorned him with wreaths of roses and golden leaves. And we all sat in a circle around him, only Little Pull was missing. He had climbed down from my shoulder and we could hear him mumbling softly with a little boy behind a large oak trunk. And the little boy looked like a goblin in his wide hood, and none of us had seen him arrive. 'If you give me your raspberry bush to give Petrus for his birthday, I will give you a little box with a little, little box inside it.' But the goblin shook his head and ate a sweet, red raspberry from his bush! 'I will give you a box,' cried Little Pull impatiently, 'with a little box inside it, and inside the little box there is an even smaller box, and inside the smaller box there is a much, much smaller box, and there is a tiny little box in the ...' Suddenly he began to cry out, for by that time the goblin had eaten all the sweet, red raspberries, then he leapt up and fled into the forest.

ON THE AFTERNOON BEFORE THE BIRTHDAY CELEBRATION, THE FOLLOWING TRANSPIRED:

The youths had not yet appeared, but Raba and Najade set the table with platters of sweet delicacies and jugs of red and golden wine and dressed the forest cottage in garlands. And the splendid birthday child and I wandered back and forth past its ivy gate. His brown eyes were two heavens, such that all who saw him – believed. And we noticed a crowd of idlers approaching; they were in heated discussion. And when they saw us, they quickened their pace, and I recognised among them those who believed themselves related to me, and they asked me to show them my son. But Raba was looking out of the little hatch of the forest cottage with a crafty smile. And when I refused, they became irascible and pelted my shame. And Petrus walked grimly among them, his beard clenched. And it transpired that Little Pull had hurried ahead of the youths, and Petrus put him on his hand and lifted him above the heads of the malicious crowd: 'You ask for the star yet you know not the heights … but here, look upon him, he has risen above your shoulders!' The youths struck the importunate enemies – only Antinous remained devoutly by my side. And then the sun returned home with its silver crossbow, and in the forest cottage we drank the red and golden wine and ate the sweet pastries. And Petrus drank from a huge, heavy goblet, a gift from his favourites which kept singing impish songs, and two of Onit von Wetterwehe's strongest Negro boys had to put it to his lips whenever Petrus was thirsty.

PETRUS PUTS LITTLE PULL IN THE SUN

And Little Pull had drunk all the frothing remnants from the goblets and secretly crept back underneath the hazelnut bush, took a deep breath and grunted as though he were sleeping. But that night Raba heard him whimper and woke me, and she put her gentle hands on my son's brow – they worked wonders. And as he lay in Raba's lap I had to sit by his side and tell him tales about all the animals, and especially the funny one about the baboon mother and her child. The two of them are sitting on a box in the cage – the baboon is holding her beautiful little baby baboon in her arms and singing:

> Sleep now, sleep now,
> My little rosy bum,
> My little sugar bun,
> My little golden bug,
> Tomorrow the Empress will come from the East
> With chocolate and bon-bons for a sugary feast,

> Quick now, quick now,
> duck down deep,
> Sweet treats come to those who sleep.

And in the morning Petrus put the pale Little Pull on a colourful hillock of flowers, and the sun played catch with him in her short fringed robe, spangled in gold.

THE CHIEFTAIN BUGDAHAN VISITS US IN THE LIMESTONE GORGE

And we sat in the limestone gorge which was like a great white cauldron and waited for Bugdahan. And Petrus called out to him, while the chieftain was struggling to climb the steep rock face: 'Welcome, Sam Bugdahan, we do not make it easy for our guests to reach us.' Yet the chieftain's cheeks were shining; his bulbous eyes were protruding from their sockets, and joy dripped from his poet's brow. His father had dug for gold in the ancient forests, and his lust for adventure had entered his son's spirit. And once he had sung his battle songs for us, Petrus said that he had heard the unmistakable sound of rusted spears creaking and the boomerang whizzing through the air. And I handed our guest a fresh drink, in a goblet carved from Australian wood in his honour. 'Beneath its flourishing shade your forefathers ate human chicken meat, Chieftain Bugdahan.' And he laughed so hard at my cannibalistic notion that Petrus and I, too, fell into riotous laughter without end. 'Maiden, you please me, would you care to keep my sister Raba company?' I stuck my tongue out at him, it got wider and redder and never did I see Petrus rejoicing so eagerly, especially as Bugdahan held me to be a joyous idol of his faith. 'You need to have a sense of humour with this one!'

And he began to stretch his stiff limbs for the journey home; puffing, he tumbled over the rock face – as he did I formed balls from earth and clay and bombarded him until he had reached the road.

PETRUS AND I IN THE TEMPLE OF JEHOVAH

Many men and women were making the steep climb from the road with their children. At the top was the Star Temple. It was the Day of Atonement for the people of Jehovah. 'Iron and yielding is our temple, sweet and sad its songs.' And Petrus said, 'Let us go up.' And the cheeks of the men and women turned pale and trembled with joy when they saw him with his shining feast-day eyes and his eternal beard. And the priest sang, and a thousand voices responded, as infinite as the ripples of the rivers of Babylon. Softly Petrus read the Hebrew chants of the Bible: 'Wondrous is the form of this ancient tongue; the characters stand like harps, and many are bowed with fine strings.' I touched his hand and pointed to the numerous silver stars on the white silk curtain: it concealed the Holy of Holies. In silence we walked side by side down the cracked stone steps of the temple into the wafting heat. On the road the birch trees tenderly reached out their branches to each other. And I picked the flowers that grew by the wayside for Petrus.

PETRUS IN THE CAVE

We could no longer stay in the mountains nor in the meadows, and the trees in the woods were like mighty pillars of ice. And we were cold and had no shelter. And the youths had fallen out with their families, who chastised them for their tarrying ways. And Onit von Wetterwehe had sailed across the seas with his personal physician Kraft and his jester. But one day Bugdahan the chieftain came to see us; he had discovered a cave near his tent. And we set out – Bugdahan in the lead, then Petrus and I; we were followed by Antinous, Najade and Grimmer von Geyerbogen as well as Goldwarth and his friend, the Jerusalemite with the consoling eyes. And we were joined by many of the other youths who were without shelter and who knew of our dwelling place. And we made a chair out of white birch wood for Petrus and upholstered it with ferns and moss. And in the morning we drew lots to choose which of our number would go out thieving during the day. And we brought home sweet cream and wheat bread which we found outside the houses of the rich, plundered great stores, and Grimmer stole a hundredweight fur for Petrus. And in the evenings we caroused; we sat around little fires, smoked pipes and drank the wines we had seized, and Petrus taught us gypsy songs.

PETRUS AND THE PHYSICIAN

Through the blank, grey sky we could clearly see the sprouting of spring blue. Petrus was lying at the edge of a forest; we had spread his great cloak beneath him. And still the youths who knew of his fevers were nowhere to be seen. Only one of them sat by his side and I at his feet, and we watched over him with concern. Antinous handed him the glowing red physic of fortified wine which he loved so dearly. But when he coughed, we anxiously looked down at our hands and smiled bashfully at each other over the mighty body as though it were a deep-breathing sea. Petrus was sleeping. 'I love you,' said Antinous, 'and I wish to kiss your eyes, they are like blackberries.' Cautiously we approached each other and hid behind the sleeping man, behind the coarse curls of his head. But having returned pensively to our positions we lifted our eyes to Petrus, and we trembled mightily at his pallor. And I ran headlong through the tall wheat; I wished to go to Raba, so she could teach me her wondrous blue spell. I would repeat it tirelessly, countless times on every pearl of my necklace, until the window of cloud above bursts open and a thousandfold warmth descends over Petrus. But the pathway that led to the steep cliffs was blocked; I had to turn back, yet I was glad to see that he was surrounded by all his favourites. And it was Onit von Wetterwehe's personal physician who was leaning over his surging chest beneath the fir branches, swaying to and fro with the fearsome thrusts of the mighty heart of Petrus: 'You cannot drive away your raw northern storm with herbs or bombard it with bitter pills, but I prescribe May rain and sun for you all!'

And Onit's Negro boys carried Petrus in a golden litter on their shoulders into the white rose garden. There the branches were already turning green and silken little birds were singing. And at midday the lithe golden woman in her radiant robe came and handed Petrus the shining goblet.

PETRUS-NOAH

Busy angel maidens spin fine silk rain without pause. We are sitting on the bank of a river sheltered by old boards which have been nailed together – Petrus raises his hand and gestures at the heavy darkness. The night woman of the West lifts two black March clouds from her blackest cellar; they look like great kettles, and there starts a howling and a terrible shrieking and blustering up above. 'That's the demons,' explains Petrus, 'and it won't be long before – boom – they send the whole damn thing down here.' And indeed, the little devils heedlessly emptied the great cloud vessels onto the ground, and the wild water flooded the meadows and the woods, and the river below us awakened and dreamed no more. And its silence seethed, and the floods grew and raised us up as high as the pine crowns of the woods all around us. The teetering ramshackle roof above us began to collapse, and my clothes were wet through, but Petrus sat and wrote about singing blossoms in the sunshine. Not a drop moistened his hand, and his beard lay like a still wave:

'My wild, black dove which I took on my journey,' said Petrus, and he smiled. And the days and nights went by, and there was no end to the playful spat. But when the little devils had tired and the maidens returned to spinning their delicate silken rain once more, I vaulted over the sunken roof of our ark and plucked young green pine cones, which we ate; but when the noisemakers splashed the water all about again, I wrapped myself in Petrus's great cloak and pressed against his lap. And then came a morning that was as sunny and serene as a great bridal chamber. The pastures sparkled with diamond droplets and the river healed and dreamed once more, and the woods were fragrant and wore new green garments and Petrus-Noah explained: spring is the faith of God, returning again and again unto the world!

PETRUS AND THE WILLOW

He sat down beneath a stunted willow tree. 'How young you are –' I said to him, and regarded the Inexpressible One beneath the grey shelter of the tree crone. How young he was in his eternity – he was Baldur, the god of jubilant light! 'Will you not come closer?' he asked me. But I was waiting for something that had no precedent. A red-cheeked storm leapt across the path and woke the sleeping crone of the roots, and she lay her two hairy, gristly branches over shiny brown ringlets. 'Spring, spring, spring is here!' Girls arrived like shimmering red and blue dragonflies and bright-eyed children with silver chimes, young sportive lambs, and they leapt and celebrated the birthday of spring. The pennants of Heaven waved blue.

PETRUS AND MAY

It is May, the Russian sage is in bloom, and there is a plant with pink flowers, and Petrus always has to tell me their names. And suddenly I was way ahead of him – he was standing in the middle of the meadow and writing. 'I shall never part from him,' I said quite loudly to the bright sky, but in his high spring spirits he didn't even hear it. But the youths had heard; their fourfold laughter resounded from a hiding place. And they lifted me over the thorn and bound me with bands of bast. 'Now you must tell us which of us Petrus loves most dearly.' I refused, so they blindfolded me and told me to reach for his heart's favourite. And I could only see a tiny droplet of morning light and beneath it Antinous, and I seized him and he clapped his long, slender hands and swept me into a boisterous dance. 'Oh, dear messenger of Petrus!' And he kissed me countless times. And then we all sat together on the fresh green, and wildly they pressed me to confess which of them I liked best – and I pointed to each of them in turn. 'Your lives play to me in notes, and I love your song like the song of songs which resounds every thousand years.' And the youths cried: 'She has drunk too much of the green air' – but I was deeply moved, and seeking to conceal my emotion, I spoke as unctuously as a preacher. And behind the fence stood Petrus, laughing and swinging his giant pencil over our heads! 'A spring with no outlet is your companion; she is a spring that rises and all at once overwhelms you.'

PETRUS AND MY LOVE

We were walking round and round the hawthorn hedges of a wondrous garden. Even my heart felt fragrant. And Petrus nodded pensively and I thought: he is a creator, the way he is always walking and smiling, smiling ... A creator, and in his great goodness he was gathering the honey of my joy for a new world, which he bore on his shoulder. Sometimes his thoughts roamed up like a flock of young birds and rested on a slender white cloud, and his eyes widened to drink in the sun, fresh from nature. But when I fell silent for a time, he looked at my lips and they rejoiced: 'I love the fair Antinous and Onit von Wetterwehe with the silken eyes and the rigid growth around his heart, and the cheeky Grimmer von Geyerbogen, and I love Goldwarth's spring hair, the twinkle of sun on his brow. But these fierce beams of infidelity often leave me pensive.' And Petrus took my hand in his and said: 'Be glad of your leaping love, it is a child and wishes to play.'

THE SORCERESS HELLMÜTE

'One must have seen them just as the mariner must have seen the lighthouse at sea,' Petrus told me, and we stepped through a long, weathered hall into the cool, round forecourt. I have only ever heard tell of tender sorceresses with golden hair; but Hellmüte was neither tender nor golden-locked; her silvery dark hair fell like heavy strands down each side of her proud face. 'Here – I bring you my comrade, I call her Tino; it is the green-red radiance of her blood – or can you tell me her older name, sorceress?' And Hellmüte kissed me on both cheeks, and when I went to show her my son, he was no longer sitting on my shoulder. All the peculiar things that were hanging from the ceiling and all the twisted grimacing beasts on the walls – Little Pull's tiny head peeked fearfully out of Petrus's great cloak pocket. But the sorceress took him from his hiding place and showed him her marabou which was standing in a corner, offended. It had been expecting green pond sweers for its name day that day, and luckily Pull had his sugar frog from the fair with him, and while the two of them became friends, an Indian boy in a leaf skirt served us white Burgundy wine. And Hellmüte's wandering sea eyes were fixed on Petrus; but he kept his head turned away and talked of sprouting islands. And the whole time we were accompanied by muted flapping music – the marabou was most entertained by my Pull, and Hellmüte asked that I should give Pull to her! His fez with the silver tassel had slipped from the bald head of his comical playmate onto its brittle beak. And when the sun joined their games, the sorceress hurried me away unseen up a spiral staircase into a wide room. 'I should like to know your older name.' Through thousand-faceted windows shone light unending. She stole a drop of blood from my heart; between light and light it clarified like a riddle. And Hellmüte pondered.

When we were on the road once more, Petrus said to me: 'Your blood predates darkness; well may the sorceress ponder your oldest name.' And we spoke to each other in that blue tongue in which Heaven and earth converse. And before us the many fields, flooded with May rain! And all three of us had the same wish – we took off our shoes, held hands and waded through the warm waters.

THE SORCERESS HELLMÜTE SENDS US GIFTS

And when Petrus saw my darkened brow, he was astonished, for the day wore a bright, merry robe and its mischievous blue eyes twinkled. I was thinking of the sorceress Hellmüte. 'It vexes me that she waits not at the shoe of your foot and that her secret dreams weave feverish sea nights about you.' But Petrus smiled: 'You are a most severe priestess.' We sat down on a bench beneath countless branches with open white umbels. And Petrus told me this bush was a stranger and that it came from the land of wondrous skies. And he took his pen and the large white scroll from his cloak pocket and wrote; but I was looking out across the wide, green lap of the meadows at the birds. They were circling through the air like silver whirlwinds – to play like that! Suddenly the sorceress Hellmüte's Indian boy was standing before us; he had come dashing through the air, the red-skinned bird with his shiny black hair adorned with bright plumage – yellow, red and green feathers. And he prostrated himself at our feet, and Petrus greeted him with all manner of cries in his mother tongue. And the young wildling shouted: *Kulaia, vivua, malibam!* And from his belt he untied a rose bush in bloom. 'Master, Hellmüte the sorceress sends this to you!' Her proud ring with the white opals lay amid the roses, but there was an aching feverish light at large in the stones. And to me she gifted sandals made of lioness hide with silver buckles. And she had not forgotten Little Pull Pasha – from now on the marabou was to be his playmate. 'But you have to hold it by the reins, Master Pull, so that it doesn't slip away like it did from me, the drifter, the glutton'; at last it came plodding slowly across the ditch. 'It was drawn by frog sirens,' said Petrus, and we went to meet it, and Pull immediately sat on the soft feathery back and rode ahead along the secluded tree-lined paths, looking around joyfully in all directions to see that we could see him! And we came to a large stubbly field; a band of boys with red apple cheeks were flying their kites, and Pull shot his pop gun at the white and red paper kites until they were all dead. And the boys marvelled at the great strange bird and kissed the brave little hunter. Petrus was glad and said: 'Never close the gate behind him, illusion is the most faithful teacher and nature the greatest classroom.' And the whole earth laughed, and great blooms of sunshine fell from the sky. That was a wonderful day! And Pull's eyes shone. And when it got dark, the marabou fell asleep at his feet, but still I had to sing him the little night song:

> Foxglove, cock's crow, glow worm
> Rambling, gambolling lambkin you
> Ambling, scrambling catkin
> Brambling shambling my own you

PETRUS AND MY CHILD

'Tomorrow I shall go to the Rhine Lands,' Petrus said to me, 'what will you do while I am away?' 'I shall take my child for a walk through the streets where the sweet sellers are.' And so we walked hand in hand through the warm air, and people passed each other by in silence. But my child was leaping at my side like a young, brown kid. At first he asked me where Petrus had gone, all alone, if he might not stir the great storm once more and all the whirling winds. Then we stopped before a sweet store; chimney sweeps, horses, dogs made of chocolate and sugar stood in the store window and all the red and green and yellow and purple bonbons … And when we went home in the evening, a great cloud man was floating in the sky above with a long, long, fluffy cloud beard; Pull recognised him immediately – and he was wearing a grey cloak – and he nodded to us and pulled the moon from a great cloud bag; it was red and round like a plump raspberry bonbon.

PETRUS AMONG THE WORKERS

We were walking through the north-east of the city, where spring cannot bloom, smothered in the narrow streets. And the children play in the courtyards, the poor with their aged faces and crooked limbs, but their little hearts are red and they wish to play and to rejoice. They placed beams criss-crossed in a pile; it gave them great squealing pleasure to fly so up-a-la up in the sky. But when they saw Petrus, they flopped back roughly onto the hard asphalt and little Lotte and little Liese howled – they believed Petrus to be the man in black. I believe he was proud of this. And at the door of the plain, grey building, Sennulf the fighter was waiting for us; he rushed to meet Petrus like one who yearns to meet his God. But the assembled workers grumbled when they saw him with his blessing eyes and shining beard. 'We don't wish to console ourselves with the Heaven of the dead; we want to have it here on earth already like the rich!' And I feared for Petrus, for some of them had clenched their coarse fists and were menacing.

But he said to me: 'Only the furtive crucify, and they cannot reach me.' And the last curses evaporated beneath Sennulf's feet. His ardent boyhood radiated a commanding chastity. 'He is a dark birch' – and his words swirled over the people hungering for liberty, like spring leaves before a thunderstorm. And at the end of the evening some of them approached Petrus, among them a poet artisan whose name was Damm. And many youths had come to see the distinguished guest: the suspicious Ludwill with the sullen violet eyes, and his friend, the scrawny, lanky painter of saints with the chiming heart, and Gorgonos the rigid. He had shimmering hair and a dead viper mouth and he hesitated to approach the Splendid One, and beside him stood his dancer, toying with his armband.

PETRUS PUTS MY PASSION TO THE TEST

(I lay a wreath of roses
on the grave of a prophet)

Two oxen were pulling our cart, and the farmer's lad was sitting on the back of the brindled horse. He had picked us up. 'Climb on and let's not be fussing!' We were weary from our journey and lay stretched out on the hard creaking boards. And when we had arrived at our destination, Petrus handed the young labourer a large bottle of brandy; 'Take a hearty swig for your trouble' – 'That be Mister Pancras? One of them ice saints? In May him and his stormy beard tore right through the seedlings.' Petrus looked icy enough, and he pointed to the quiet garden of the Prophet where white mulberry trees and milk vetch bushes enclosed the domed temple like a rustling wall. 'His forefathers roamed mountains in the highlands of Iran,' said Petrus, 'and in the clouds he formed the new breed of man out of the laughing midday sun of his homeland. Verily a divine sculptor

– and whosoever wishes to be reflected in the eye of his creation must have wings like his.' I listened devoutly, for the words of Petrus resounded like a rite. And around my arm he put the wreath of red roses – we had had it made in a nursery on the road; it was still shining brightly with joyful midday glow. And he put a dagger in my belt – I knew not why. But when I passed through the golden gate into that place, it was sweet vanities that wafted towards me rather than the dry, petrified air of thousand-year-old royal tombs – cats crept over their edges like light-lost slumber. And I was overcome with loathing and wrath when I saw the prophet's cat; she was crouched on his dead heart as though it were a soft silk pillow – her back had been a footstool for his weary feet. And when I returned to Petrus, my body was aflame, and from my belt he drew the dagger, which was dripping blood. And as my hands showed no traces, he said: 'You shall prepare a throne for my remembrance.'

PETRUS YEARNING

Hemmed in by hedges, the fields cannot spread, and the young waters are trapped by dams. 'I feel as they do, Petrus, that is why I am sad. But once on an autumn evening, you and the youths poured lathering gold from Heaven – I was lying at a distance behind the gardens in the open meadow. And the storms were calling like wild birds, and my soul cast off all that was feeble, and I hurried, over your head, over the seas of your reverence, through the rose realms of your tenderness, until I came to rest on the summit of your heart. You godly drinker, I was once the drink of your drunkenness.'

PETRUS REMINDS ME

'We have wandered a starry life together already,' – Petrus reminded me – 'and you never called my name.' And I said: 'To every cloud at night, to every day I called your name, and the sun has embroidered an altar for it … and one day a life will surround me with people like walls, all wishing to hear your name. And my voice shall be an ocean. Your name is the name of the world!' Petrus nodded, and when I looked up at him, innumerable firmaments shone from his face and it was without end, and I had to turn away that I should not be blinded. But I felt my strength as it pushed outward, and I reared and stretched, and I kept my eyes open before that abundance of majesty.

PETRUS PUTS A FARMER'S SON BACK IN THE EARTH

The sky is sparkling like a ripe field of corn. Petrus and I are lying in the shade of a maple tree. It is early autumn and the air is still simmering on the stove of summer. We are both thinking of the harvest festival, and I swing around in circles a thousand times like a couple rollicking at the dance. And I feel compelled to imitate the peasant brothers, how they blow their potato noses. 'But these cursing beasts of burden are robust, they have no souls to bother them.' Men approached down the narrow track; they were carrying pitchforks, scythes and other tools on their backs, preceded by a shaggy dog sniffing the air. 'Well, on this glorious night you might well curse, I'll give you that.' The coarsest had opened his great damn mouth again, but the old wrinkled farmer warned him. 'I'll come at your ribs,' adding mysteriously, 'That is one of the apostles.' And he went on, 'him with the big beard could probably tell him,' he said, pointing to his six sons, 'where to find the seventh of the six out walking. He always had his head stuck in the clouds, got it from his mother you know, she knew all of the plants and all of the birds, but she didn't want to know anything about the menfolk and the womenfolk, and her work went its own way, softly softly. Yesterday evening she creeps up to my bed with that coffin face; like a saint she looks and she says: "Gustav is dead". Three times she said it so it's got to be true.' 'Of course it must be true,' said Petrus, and the six sons crept behind the leaves of the maple tree. But he called to the brothers and approached them. The sheaves stood upright like golden sacks, only a few lay upended on the bristly stretch of grain. 'Farmer, you are truly a Croesus,' cried Petrus, and the six sons suddenly made an effort to speak properly while the old man kept repeating with his worn-out bagpipe falsetto: 'Gustav, Gustav my chickadee, cluck, cluck, cluck, cluck!' 'The way his conscience afflicts him, he must share some of the blame.' And as we came to the third field, the shaggy dog knocked over some of the sheaf sacks, sniffing the pale gold, licking them and whining like a child. And Petrus leaned over the pale golden body. 'Farmer, here is your seventh son. Gold amidst the gold of autumn.' And I asked Petrus to wake him. But he shook his head gravely. 'Farmer, your son is dead' – and turning to the six: 'Your brother was a poet.' And the trembling breath which yet shimmered over the dead son melted away. 'But tell us, what is the name of the man with the coarse beard?' Petrus nodded at me to deflect the question, but I said to the brothers: 'His name is the name of the world.' And the old farmer with the bobbing head said: 'I said it right from the start, he is not one of us.' Petrus asked that the dead boy be brought to him and he laid him down beneath the parting day. But when darkness fell he put him on his shoulder, covered his body with the collar of his cloak, and strode down the village hill. The evening slumbered between the folds of his brow, and I followed the great archangel who covered the Misunderstood One with his wing. After three days, Petrus himself laid him back in the ground.

PETRUS AND THE EMERALD

Before us the lake shimmered in green splintered rays. We were sitting on a low gravel hill and letting the little things slip through our fingers. 'Look what I have found here!' cried Petrus – he was holding a transparent stone in his hand and assessing its purity. 'I found an emerald! You lucky little rogue, I'll have it capture you in its rays.' But I suggested to Petrus that it would be better to sell it and celebrate the midsummer day with golden oak mead. And we hurried into the town. Petrus had already laid the gem between my two hands, carefully, as though he were placing it in a jewel box. The merchant's window sparkled with diadems and strands of coloured gems and sweet white pearl rings, and apprehensively I followed him into the jeweller's shop and I felt timid when the curious assistants asked us what we wanted. But Petrus triumphantly placed the precious find on the flat of his hand. 'I found it among gravel but I could not have set it more radiantly in the crown of a queen in one of my stories. But I should like to ask your master himself if he wishes to purchase it.' The man had already seen it glowing from a distance and put it to a stringent test. It stood out beautifully against the brown velvet of his sleeve. 'This is a precious jewel that you bring me, Master; if you are satisfied with ten gold pieces, shall we agree?' Crouched behind the glass cabinets and behind the counters, the assistants were trying to conceal their laughter, while their master kept delighting anew in the blaze of the emerald. And when we were standing before the shop window once more, Petrus smiled and put the ten gold pieces in my hands, 'for the oak-mead golden solstice.' But before we reached the bend in the road I turned around again and saw the gallant goldsmith, standing at the door of his gold shop surrounded by merry faces.

OUR OAK MEAD GOLDEN SOLSTICE CELEBRATION

A woolly carpet of moss, embroidered with blue and red berries, is laid across the forest floor, and the last Nordic spring shoot has donned its summer crown. Men, half-naked, carry barrels full of mead on their broad backs and young boar rams from Onit von Wetterwehe's hunts on spits, and plant their spears and tools in our our green hall. And Raba and Najade, a dark fairy and a blond fairy, sit at the edge of the forest, weaving garments from ferns and silken grasses, and tying garlands of oak leaves and wild roses and a mighty wreath for Petrus-Odin's head; his beard hangs over his angular chest like a sunny pasture. And Little Pull sits on my shoulder and calls out his colourful notions to the youths. Setting across streams and hedges they approach, clad in bearskins. Antinous looks like an enchanted mythical king, his brother's curls are bursting yellow, and Onit's eyes hurry ahead like lean hounds at hunt. And Goldwarth strides before the band of hornblowers, and wood sprites carrying laughing elves in their arms leap about on both sides of the forest paths, and Tabak is among their number; yet the little forest maidens resist his embrace – he is unclean and they are all wearing enchanted white morning silk. But Gorgonos the rigid gazes impassively – his dancer prances around him in lemon satin folds, precious rings glittering in his ears. And he is followed by the nobles, knights and dames on magnificent steeds and the ruby-eyed twins singing side-by-side in silver saddles. Weißgerte's eyes are as wide as secrets. But Bugdahan's clumsy feet stumble over the hunched tree roots, and his father, the aged chieftain, is riding a bullock beside him. His left arm hangs limply over the neck of the powerful beast. Enemy tribes had been holding the fearsome warrior hostage, tied to a coconut tree. And when he saw Petrus-Odin, he wept with delight. And Petrus-Odin asked him to bless me. And Goldwarth had brought his mother, who had the grace of a maiden, and Petrus said to her: 'Mistress Emmelei, you are so very young, you could have been with your son in the cradle.' And whenever Petrus-Odin lifted his arms to raise the storm, the fanfares thundered. And the youths built altars from felled trunks and branches and sent up sacrificial smoke. And the elves played ring-a-ring-a-roses around Petrus-Odin and the wood sprites did their teasing. And I had to dance with the dancer in butterfly yellow – we were mere breath. And the golden drizzle of mead frothed in the mighty tankards, and we ate the game roasted on the spit. But Petrus-Odin was missing Ben Ali Brom, the Jerusalemite. Raba, the sister of the chieftain, began to weep bitterly; Bugdahan had beat his pale cheeks and torn off his beard, for his fathers in Jerusalem preferred shame to death.

And we shook with joy and the whole forest shook with us, and Gorgonos the rigid laughed more than he ever had at the antics of his dancer.

And once the day had rushed by, Petrus-Odin told us the legends of the north and prophesied, and it transpired: as one of his eyes was extinguished by darkness, the other was filled and shone twice as bright – a midnight sun. And we all lay about him on the soft forest floor and slept.

MY DREAM

In the morning, when Petrus-Odin and the knights and the noble ladies and their squires, the elves and wood sprites lay in a deep mead slumber, my eyes closed as well and I dissolved into a green gold medley. – And stretched across the forest floor, he lay there, a giant oak with a leafy head as old as stars. Giggling elves danced twisting-twigling around him and tugged at his shining beard, and a horde of wood sprites had gathered on his chest to buck, and a tiny little wood sprite which was carrying a little buttercup wound around its little rosy stalk hid in Petrus-Odin's great ear – it was my Pull.

PETRUS AND THE JERUSALEMITES

Several days after the great feast of Odin, Ben Ali Brom and the other Jerusalemites visited us; they had been in their homeland once more and brought gifts for Petrus and me – changes of raiment and silk scarves, carved boxes and jewellery made of cedar wood, and candied red roses and other sweets. And they came barefoot, like pilgrims. And Petrus spoke many sunlit words with them. But the youths hurried up from the forest, they had heard the wishes of the Jews and feared that Petrus would grant them and lead them on to the lost land of their fathers. But he answered them: 'Whosoever carries not his homeland within him, yet shall it grow beneath his feet.' But the youngest of the strangers put his turban on me, and a sorrow came over my life, like the cloud of sadness over the golden sky, and my hands yearned to play with stars. 'Look, the eyes of your companion are cast to the east,' cried the Jerusalemites. And Petrus wavered, but his favourites were laughing at their divine cunning – and they secretly took their harps and played harsh sounds on them rather than the sweet songs of the lands of Sabaoth. And Petrus scolded them. And the two of us withdrew to the mountains and sat atop the peaks as though we were riding great dromedaries. His beard waved – a pennant for a king. And in the distance we saw the youths heading home, heads raised defiantly; to their right and left went the poets in turbans, their gestures bespeaking wonders.

PETRUS AND I IN THE MOUNTAINS II

The next morning we were veiled in clouds. And down at the foot of the mountains we saw the youths and the two maidens Raba and Najade. But Petrus was playing with a little dewdrop; it glistened on the surface of his Zeus hand like a beetle made of mother-of-pearl, like a sweet little soul, a trembling dancer – dreaming all the while … a tender gold-foot gently expiring. 'At least it had some life that way, even if it was afraid of my cruel hand,' Petrus said, seeking to console me, for it lay on the hard stones and was dead. But deep in the mountains there was thunder at the blue Zeus lightning veins of his brow. And around the mountains lay the weary youths and the two noble maidens, like young gods and goddesses of love.

PETRUS AND I IN THE MOUNTAINS III

Goldwarth was leaning against the rock face down by the lake, playing his fiddle; the others had left as the day expired. 'He loves you,' said Petrus, 'he is a boy in his armour and he shall defy all your storms.' And the first star rose like a trembling silver ring, and the faithful fiddler's yearning, fragrant melody floated up to us wreathed around the evening wind. And then suddenly seemed to sink into the lake.

PETRUS AND I IN THE MOUNTAINS IV

Above us the sunset bled like a battlefield of fallen warriors; but the gentle night bowed in consolation over the red, dying clouds, and its great golden eye was seeking God. 'Why did He create Himself without form, why did He do that?' 'So that He would not be constricted and confined,' said Petrus, 'and He spreads over everything.' And we climbed the steps of the cloud, and Petrus taught me the names of the many stars which lit up when he pointed to them. And I shouted bright sounds of jubilation at the ground – my human disguise wafted away. And I turned wild when Petrus said he wished to go back down to the ground with me. 'I no longer wish to be among hearts.' But he reminded me of Antinous and his love for me and the blond, rosy-locked rogue Grimmer. 'And what would the princely host say, and how would Goldwarth's fiddle lament? You must give them a thousand hands to the rose dance around the day and yearn for the meadows at night. All about you must be in bloom if, like me, once satisfied, you would drink of life.' And I grasped his hand and hid my face. The rejoicing boys were godly desires and a drop of his eternity, like me. The pastures and forests slumbered in their green, beyond them was the starving city, a terrible maw of grey buildings with sharp turrets. And Petrus pointed to the starving city and assured me: 'For my sake, it shall not tear you apart.'

PETRUS AND I IN THE MOUNTAINS V

In the city the news spread that Petrus and the boy (as they called me) had been struck by lightning that night up in the mountains. And all who knew of him gathered, along with many more who were avid to see him. And when they saw him alive on the heights, they sounded great horns and launched rockets into the sky, which resounded amid the blue in multicoloured stars. But the face of Petrus was increasingly creased and averted, and it was as though it were growing up into the sky and his beard were rising above the world. And I lay like a ring around his foot, which was as stone. And Petrus addressed the noisy crowd, yet I did not hear his words over the roar of his voice; but the people down by the waters were listening, spellbound, and long after there was a sinister rustling in the the woods all around:

> The evening rests on my brow,
> Human I heard not your murmurs,
> Heard not the roaring of your heart –

And is your heart not the deepest shell on earth!
Oh, how I dreamed of that earthen tone.
Listened for the ringing of your joy,
I reclined on your apprehension and hearkened,
But dead is your heart and forsaken.
Oh, how I yearned for that earthen tone …
Coolly the evening presses it to my brow.

PETRUS AND I IN THE MOUNTAINS VI

For three days and three nights we sat up there, and at times flocks of wild geese would fly past us and storms chased each other up above; where were they rushing to? And we felt no yearning for the valley, but our skin was burnt brown and our lank hair drooped over our shoulders, and we yearned for rain like the ground on which we sat. And Petrus cast off his grey cloak for the first time, and I saw how narrow his shoulders were, yet how mighty his rearing head, like a call from on high above the earth. 'Who are you talking to, Petrus?' His lips were moving softly, facing west. 'I am talking to the distant one who will guide me.' And then he asked me: 'What will you do if I should wander on another star?' And when Petrus saw how sad I was, he bowed his head and told me dreams and fairy tales from the cities of the Golden Mother.

PETRUS AND I IN
THE MOUNTAINS VII

Most of all I loved hearing about the city of the lagoon, my mother's favourite city; comforting scents would stir and gently rock me. Her ancestors who bore the mark of David had been guests of the Doges long ago. 'Sometimes it seems to me,' said Petrus, 'that you have the same eyes as my deepest dream.' It was written on his heart with my mother's celestial letters, and the gondoliers still tell the foreign passengers about it when they gondola past St. Mark's Square. San Marco stands before his cathedral. The gold-veined marble palm at his feet had fallen from his hand when he stepped from his niche to bless the foreign Signora. The sky hung over the waggish will of the city like a blue velvet baldachin. 'And in the evening the stars told each other,' said Petrus, 'per omnia saecula saeculorum.' And his gaze plunged a thousand leagues deep. Stiff folds enveloped him, and he was nothing but form and no longer a body. I had seen him like this once before in the first bloom of my blood, merely felt him with a hearkening heartbeat, enveloped in silken skin amid tender nights. And I was afraid; he was a sorcerer, and I fell down the mountains, my heart racing ahead, over the meadows and hedges, and my head was a tower; I was lost to myself – – – – – – – – – – – – – –

It was in the late spring of 1903 that fear drove me away from the eldest of the earth.

THE YOUTHS FIND ME
AT THE HEDGE

I was lying before a hedge and the youths were standing in a circle around me and whispering and wondering why Petrus was not with me. And when I opened my eyes I was looking into pale faces. 'Why is your hair dishevelled and your robe torn?' And when I did not answer, Goldwarth put his velvet cloak beneath my head, lay me down and caressed my trembling hands. And Antinous wept. And then Bugdahan, the bandit, came and said to them: 'She has fallen into melancholy; her lips, which were open on the midsummer day, are tightly closed. Hurry to the Shining One and tell him that he should not tarry, for the soul of his companion is falling into the most terrible abyss.' In the meantime, he went and fetched his sister Raba, who brought me a tea of wondrous healing herbs from her homeland and on my breast placed a star of metal which she said banishes all evil. And Antinous's sister Najade came and her arms cradled me like the silken winds of May. But my blood remained mute and my heart was blind. And the evening looked upon the earth with a veiled eye, and at last we saw the youths who had gone to fetch Petrus approaching; but he was not with him, and their heads hung like withered fruit on their chests.

GOLDWARTH COMFORTS ME IN MY MELANCHOLY

A blow! And I recognised the voice of Petrus; the thunderous word was still rumbling down the ridge of the world. And the youths rejoiced when they looked into my eyes again. Grey canvas hung over us like a screen, and the kindling was burning, for the night was bare and its breath was cool! Najade arose and reminded Antinous: 'Our sisters fear for us, and the path there lies far beyond the meadows.' And Raba spoke of her old, troubled father, who could not sleep, 'and already the early star is singing its chiming song.' And the white pennant arms waved from Onit von Wetterwehe's castle. Princess Weißgerte was standing before the gate and blowing her golden hunting horn. 'Farewell, Tino, greet the Shining One!' And the other youths followed it. And when Bugdahan, the bandit, saw that my eyes did not wish to release them, he said: 'Maiden, friendship is a word for frogs!' But Goldwarth sat quietly by my side. 'Do you not have anyone who calls to you?' And he kissed my cheek and said: 'I cannot hear their calling over your silence!' But Bugdahan warned him and looked at the two of us sorrowfully. 'Oh youth, if not for the shine of your golden hair, things would not be well for you!' I felt myself engulfed in tombs once more.

I SEARCH FOR HIM

But when morning came and Goldwarth broke into a garden to pick flowers for me, I struggled to my feet and fled across the broad meadows. And I did not rest until I saw the mountains and him at the peak. I called, but there was a muffled echo and all at once I felt that I would never reach him again. Whenever I stood on the mountains, he was walking in the valley, and at times I fancied the valley was walking around him, and when I stepped over the sharp stones down into the valley, he was up on high. And I searched for his voice for my feet were already bleeding. Finally, late one evening, I heard my name called out – and then: 'Maiden who seeks me, the deepest of my heartbeat, I have had a difficult journey, from world to world, it shall not be long before I reach the heavenly star.' I kept listening for a long time after, but the fog between us came down heavier and heavier.

TWO GREAT ANGELS CARRY PETRUS INTO THE VALLEY

I sat by the water and wet my face, and the little ripples toyed with my weary hands and feet. I had not seen Petrus for days, and I knew that he had alighted on the blue shore. And two men asked me the way to the city; they were carrying a bier and had grave, wavering eyes. I sensed who they were bearing and bowed before the Shrouded One. But when I saw the bier bearers in the distance, I cried so loudly – and the lake stood still; the spring winds froze and the sky fell upon the world in savage tears. And I rent my garments and hid my fearful face in the ground.

AT MIDDAY

And my heart was like a great coffin, but a storm arose and tore the young leaves of the woods and shook the rocks, and their peaks swayed terribly. And my hair flew like a mourning veil over the lake, on and on, until it covered the roofs of the city. Two arms embraced me in consolation; they bore broken chains – it was Sennulf the fighter. From the dungeon window he had seen the men with the grave, wavering eyes pass by and recognised the sleeping countenance of the Most Splendid One through the thick linen. And in the distance I saw the youths hurrying towards me, they had not expected to find me at the foot of the mountain. And we kissed each other on the mouth and wept.

IN THE EVENING

In the evening two red-cheeked children came from over the mountains, striding along the lake. The boy was carrying an enormous pencil and the girl a mighty scroll of paper, and they were delighting in their precious find. I let them keep them, for Petrus loved the little ones.

I SMITE TABAK

On the morning of the funeral I saw Tabak the fool; he was grinning, and his lips were bright green. And in his hand he was holding a wreath, and in place of roses there were small candles between the blossoms. 'Petrus must wear this around his neck on his pilgrimage to Heaven, for an eclipse of the moon is prophesied for this evening.' The youths who had been slowly walking behind me had heard his loose talk and turned pale, yet they bowed in silence before the melancholy morn. But I strode on in haste, ahead of that green mouth. I lured him behind the bushes; the sky burned angry red between the leaves, and I raised my fist, which was steeled by summer lightning, and smote him and hastily covered him in earth and branches.

PETRUS'S GRAVE

And multitudes came from all directions, men who knew Petrus and those who had only seen him, and women who had met him – they were all in mourning. But we had put on our festive garments, for Petrus only ever spoke of the joyful death which walks hand in hand with life. And his favourites stood on the mound before his open grave and behind them was Kraft, the personal physician, and Bugdahan with his aged father. And the maidens and the youths who had danced around him like an ancient stone idol knelt in reverence. And the cavaliers came and the princesses from the feast of Onit von Wetterwehe; Weißgerte and the twin princesses wept. And King Otteweihe had returned from the ocean; he had seen the cloud of premonition passing in the sky. And Gorgonos the rigid leaned against his dancer, and Ben Ali Brom and the other Jerusalemites prayed. And I recognised Ludwill and the painter of saints with his ringing simplicity and Damm, the artisan, and many more from the plain grey building in the south-east of the city, who grumbled when they saw Petrus. But I was standing far from the grave. And still they came – wanderers, rich and poor on crutches, entering the quiet garden with its great monuments, with its stone trunks which neither blossom nor wither. And I thought: how often he must have withered, since he blossomed into the sky so full of luminous life. My eyes were closed tight, but I felt Raba's hand on mine and Najade's warm breath. And Hellmüte, the sorceress, held me in her arms and gazed anxiously into my face. I heard glass angels singing over the cool garden until his shroud lay in the grave.

HIS NAME IS THE NAME OF THE WORLD

And when the last of them had left the cool garden and were walking home through the smiling Petrus weather, I took my leave of the youths. 'Should one of us not accompany you?' They knew I would be drawn back to the throne of the mountains. And I stayed for three days and three nights. At night I gazed at the greatest star, the blessed, golden temple, and in the day I waited for the night. And only once did someone approach the mountains (I knew him not); but when he reached me, he asked if he could kiss my brow, for it bore his image. But I pointed to the mossy rock on high atop which Petrus had so often rested. The stranger fell down before it and prayed in the tongue of his homeland. And on the morning of the fourth day I strode down from the mountains and many heavy boulders fell behind me, and once more I took the path that led to his grave. Beneath the white dream robe of morn a band of dancing devils encircled his grave, and when they saw me they tried to hide. But I motioned for them to end their obsequies; they were the faithful Negro boys of Onit von Wetterwehe. The wreaths of the mourners were still blooming on the grave, and the flowers from Raba and Najade were full of tears, and the wreath of his favourites was as fragrant as a flower bed – it bore a white silk bow – and on it in gold letters were the words: To the Jubilant Prophet. And I wrote in the earth:

His name is the name of the world.

THE NIGHTS OF TINO OF BAGHDAD

This book I give to my beloved
playmate, Sascha
(Senna Hoy)

I DANCE IN THE MOSQUE

You must visit me three days after the rainy season, for the Nile has receded then, and great flowers shine in my gardens, and I too rise from the earth and breathe. A mummy am I, as old as stars, and I dance in the time of the leas. Solemn is my eye and prophetic rises my arm, and above my brow the dance draws a slender flame and it pales and reddens again from my bottom lip to my chin. And the colourful beads around my neck all jangle ... oh, *machmêde macheiï* ... the glow of my foot is yet here, gently my shoulders twitch – *machmêde macheiï*, my loins rock my body all the while like a dark golden star. Dervi, dervish, a star is my body. *Machmêde macheiï*, my lips ache no more ... my blood trickles intoxicating sweet and dreaming, dreaming rises my finger – mysterious, like the stem of the Allah blossom ... *Machmêde macheiï*, my face fanning back and forth – lashing out as swift as a viper, and my dance catches on the stone ring in my ear. *Machmêde macheiï, machmêde machmêde* ....

THE BLUE CHAMBER

And for some days now my crown has begun to tremble, I feel a slight burning on my brow, and my eyes are half closed. My sadness knows no limit, it feels as though it might overwhelm me, like dull weeping mist overwhelms a city. My dark-skinned slaves stand around me like black marble pillars, and always love stands before my soul as though before a temple. The Khedive orders festivities for my amusement … pipers and flute players play bright, green music. Jugglers in dishevelled flax wigs scamper up narrow steps with feline agility, climb swaying bamboo poles and vault across the archery field of the palace. The cup-bearer and the food-servers wear crocodile masks, and jesters with brightly painted hands and feet turn circles in their wild, wide, bell-spangled skirts. But my eyes are half closed, and the hard red stones of my crown melt away – and my slender slaves bend like pine trees and secretly harken to the fever of my millennial heart. And when you are here in the homeland again, Senna Pasha, you shall read my name in hieroglyphs on the face of the Great Pyramid.

Senna Pasha – – – I am sitting on the bed of roses behind the silver gables of the palace and looking across – over a forest of Pharaoh trees ... – – under the great shining dome lies the harem, and I stare at the window of my abandoned chamber and its blue walls. The ambassador's heavy standard rises like an alien, defensive hand beside the proud, shining dome. My sadness knows no end – – I feel as though I were suffocating beneath a desert of sand. Never have I loved a princess or a prince as I loved my blue chamber. It embraced me like a mother, rocking me in its blue arm and never was there a king who had deeper blue eyes of an evening than my noble blue chamber. A blue swan it was, and I glided upon it – – a four o'clock flower it was, my sweet blue chamber – ay, a dancer ... her steps silken blue ... soft as spells ... and it danced bright shadows with the sun and wrapped blue dreams around the stars, and have you ever seen a chamber with blue hair, Senna Pasha? Oh, a kiss it was my blue chamber and I die of that blue, blue kiss. And my timid slaves embrace each other in their sleep – I sing airs of mortal notes. All the stars cover my face ... – – – – – –

Oh my blue murmuring garden, oh my lost blue night ... By the Great Prophet, Senna Pasha, keep my secret in your heart.

PLUMM PASHA

When Plumm Pasha came to Baghdad, he saw my son Pull in the courtyard of the palace riding a white elephant with his playmates behind him, riding along the wall mosaic, riding over the green and blue stones of the forecourt. But then Pull beheld the prince and at his signal the little Bedouins sprang from the backs of their giants and threw themselves at the feet of the venerable guest. Plumm Pasha is the most genial prince of Egypt, he delighted in my son's haughty game and approached him with all due ceremony as though approaching the Khedive himself. Graciously my son laid his chain of young crocodile teeth around his neck and let the smiling prince lift him off the saddle and kiss him on both cheeks. 'His limbs are ivory. I should like to have him here with me in the blossom season in my palace at the cataracts.' – Some time later we receive an invitation from Plumm Pasha. I have raiments made for Pull, yellow India silk with pearl-embroidered braiding, and over his brown hair he wears a dark blue fez with a long silver tassel. 'His limbs are ivory,' Plumm Pasha said, and Pull complains because they are not sugar. But the genial prince sends us small sailing boats laden with sweetmeats to welcome us, and he himself stands before the gate of his garden to receive my son. Through the wide rooms of the palace he carries him on his shoulders and neighs like one of the stallions in the stables. He lets him tousle his fluttering hair, takes him on trips down the Nile, and feeds colourful bonbons to the large Khedive fish for his amusement. But the young princes in the harem fear Pull's tyranny; he beats them when they fail to do his bidding, and the sweet princesses cry. He has hidden all their dolls behind the alcoves again. Plumm Pasha does not stop him, and the women of the harem cast disapproving glances at my son. And as of yesterday he wears the Order of the Golden Elephant with its ruby eye on his chest, and this means that all must accord him the honour due a pasha. And the genial prince has betrothed him to his twin princess daughters, who are one and a half years old and have no hair. But they always want to play with Pull's long silver tassel. – In Baghdad, colourful painted fringed carpets hang from the roofs for our arrival, and the city is decked with garlands. And Plumm Pasha grows more melancholy every day, and soon I shall surely have to decide whether to remain in his palace at the cataracts and become his seventy-ninth wife …………

ACHED BEY

Ached Bey is the Caliph, and I am Tino and I dwell in the palace of my uncle. From a small dome window I can observe him when he lies on his roof and awaits the night. His beard rests atop Baghdad, and as each new star rises in the sky, a fold of his wrinkled brow vanishes. Weary desert travellers ride past the palace on dromedaries – *cha machalâa!!* … the drowsy sound of the caravan. My uncle, the Caliph, greets them with his great hand. Meanwhile I pass through secret passageways over weathered stone floors past forgotten idols – I should like to fight with their fearsome talons, but I am drawn by the scent of the black Naomi rose on his roof. Naomi … everyone at the court knows of the Jewess of his youth. My uncle, the Caliph, raises his great hand; the black fan-bearers and Sudan Negroes obey his command, only the oldest of the palace servants humbly approaches his ear (I am unveiled), but my uncle, the Caliph, waves him away with his great hand. We smoke opium from velvet-draped pipes and drink blue liquid from diamond vessels, and I bend over the hieroglyphs of his great hand. The next morning my slave girls dress me in boy's clothes, and I carry his dagger with the emerald-studded handle in my belt, and we ride on great grey beasts to the forecourts where the traitors of the land are beheaded … My uncle, the Caliph, reclines between two marble pillars on a pillow of stigmatic red, and he raises and lowers his great hand to signal the blood penalty of death. Beheaded sons of noble Mohammedan house lean against infidels, only the head of the young stranger remains defiantly on its neck. Three times they bring him, and three times they – the snarling executioners – return him to barred night. My uncle's great hand flits into my lap, but I cannot interpret the rising hieroglyphs in the beating of his pulse. Finally he lowers his great hand. The stranger's blood drips through the cracks of the stone gates, across the rough, broad stones of the courtyards, right up to the Caliph's feet. Never did I hear a more eternal stream. It sings like the Jehovah priests on their high holy days, like the Moses summit of Sinai.

My uncle, the Caliph, lies dead in the palace on his great hand.

In the mosques the dervishes pray and whirl in their sparkling mourning garments, dark stars orbiting his soul. And the next day the mourning women come and wail, and before the palace stand black-haired women who offer holy wares, cats with golden gleaming fur (for the tomb of the Caliph); the drowsy eyes of the animals are the colour of the Naomi rose. And Jews are advancing on Baghdad, boys with melancholy eyes and girls, wild black doves, and they cast stones at the grave of the stranger – and as they move along the road they curse and wave their fists before the palace of my uncle, the Caliph. He dwells with Allah, but I see the Jew wandering all about … his stride is as the stone beneath him, but his lips are parted, rosy poet's lips like the lips of the tyrant when he lay on the roof thinking of Naomi, the Jewess of his youth.

All of my black pearls are sunken like caverns – the dark heads of my ancestors hang from my tiara. My lips are dead, but from my eyes rise pillars of fire, they follow the tails of all the stars, his singing blood – I dance, dance a dance unending which draws a dark cloud over Baghdad, I dance over the waves of the seas, stir up the sand of the desert, and before the palace the people are listening and the Jewish boys and girls fall silent ....

THE TEMPLE OF JEHOVAH

And I pulled my golden shoes from my feet, and my steps were bare. And I climbed to the top of the mountain that looks down upon the drunken city. And as I sang to the nights, the gold of the stars fell into my lap – and I built a temple for Jehovah from the eternal light of Heaven. Arch birds sit atop its walls, winged figures, and seek their songs of paradise. And I am a mummy dancing before its portal ....

MINN, THE SON OF THE SULTAN OF MOROCCO

The Sultan of Morocco wears a cloak of white silk, fastened across his chest with an emerald the size of a dove's egg. But his son is barefoot and shrouded in a dusty camel skin, a beggar beside his royal father. My cousin in the camel skin is sixteen years old, Ali Mohammed could be his older brother; he is never given to ire, always to jest, he has beautiful teeth, mother-of-pearl, sweet womanly teeth, and he smiles at his son's dour spirits. And the furrow between his brows is but a rare, fluttering shadow; the night slumbers in his son's forehead seven skins deeper. At the table the courtiers refuse to sit beside him, and on the roof his pillow is marked anxiously. Under the mellow sky of the white rose garden he strolls forbidden paths; only we women may stroll amid its white scent. But I beg permission from my father, the white-bearded Pasha, to dance with my cousin in the camel hair on the day of the coronation. And I dance with Minn, the Sultan's foolish son. My hands are crossed, my fingers spread, a pale golden star spread athwart his ragged chest. 'Now I must hurry from the feast,' says my cousin sadly, 'for you shall not wish to dance with me again.' Vexed, I ask if he believes me to suffer such foolish humours as he, then I follow him on the tips of my ringed toes to the great pool in the dark court of the Sultan. 'Minn, do you see me, am I not your dancer?' And as he says nothing, I say contemptuously, 'I should like to know if they are heroes' shoulders hidden beneath your cloak, or if my dreams mock me and that your arms could not even tame a kitten?' 'Oh, I am a thousand times stronger than your dreams tell, my proud Princess, because I wear this poor garment and remain even-tempered in the face of staring contempt. Methinks I am the strongest hero in the land.' He tugs at the shaggy seam of his coat, a stitch unravels and the entire pelt falls to the ground. Tenderly, gently, the evening colours his limbs. 'Will you dance with me once more as a reward for casting off my armour? Listen to the piping tones of the roses in the white garden, singing in our honour.' Slaves find us – and they hesitate – the women are sitting on the edge of the great pool, their faces outstretched, and behind the palm stand our fathers, Sultan Ali Mohammed and Mohammed Pasha, his older, white-bearded brother. We dance until our feet are one in turning. Then the black servants, whose naked eyes have beheld our naked dance, my body and above all my face, have their tongues speared on my father's orders, and he has the noble courtiers blinded in the forecourt of the palace; the princesses are spared punishment as they only beheld the prince. Each day he receives gifts from them, arm bands, girdles, and on the roof lie embroidered silk pillows for his dreams. The wife of the fruit decorator gives him a transparent fig leaf carved from moonstone. But the fluttering shadow on his royal father's brow claws deep into his flesh, and glowering he scowls about the palace until it is light. It is thought that he broke one of his mother-of-pearl teeth on a pillar in shock that night. It is no longer his gaze the women of the harem yearn for from the windows of their chambers, rather it is for the sake of his son that they bribe the eunuchs who find men's garments for them so that they may sit at the table for the evening meal. I keep my eyes lowered over the mournful rose garden; dazzling flattery has caused Minn to forget the sacred night of dance. Only my father lets his white beard glide over my hands at times, and says nothing. He believes I thought it all a dream. But the roses in the white garden have turned grey. Minn lies gnawed beneath broken branches. The gardeners say, 'only a jealous princess could have been so cruel.' I know who rent his tender, gentle limbs – my chamber shone green with the emerald on the silk cloak as it passed – his father, the Sultan of Morocco.

THE FAKIR OF THEBES

'Innahu gad marâh alleiya alkahane fi siyab …'
Priests in white robes were walking along the road to Thebes; I bowed before their holy presence and asked them to take me in their midst. And the pious men smiled benignly, only the Fakir, who had been buried several times already and had gathered the powers of the earth, furrowed his brow when I presented my request. He hated women, and destroying them was one of his pious works. But he noticed the ring on my finger with its rare caelum stone. It came from the treasure of a defeated warrior from Latinium. The caelum changed colour with the hour of the sky. In the morning it glowed with a dreamlike silver tint, at midday it was all sweet purple melancholy, then as it was enveloped in twilight it darkened with the night in countless stars. The Fakir stared intently at my ring and mumbled unintelligible words. I was afraid. When we reached Thebes and the women saw their Fakir in the company of the other priests, their bodies quivered as though they were in

childbed. Many of them dropped their jugs and hurried back to their homes, for any woman the Fakir touched with his fleshless hand would bleed for forty days. And it was as a plague whenever he appeared; soon a quarter of the city's healthiest women were bleeding. Still in the company of the priests, I walked beside him and the cruel holy man spared me – he gazed at my ring, at its stone; it was glad, shining as brightly as the sky over Thebes. But I was much afflicted by the fate of the city, and as none of its inhabitants ventured to approach the Fakir, I fell down before him, clutched his cold foot and implored him not to sacrifice any more of my sisters to his pious works. Avidly he gazed at my ring, at the beautiful stone in which I carried the sky. This he demanded in exchange for his mercy. Stubbornly I shook my head, and that same day all the women in the city bled. And it was as a gruesome sea over Thebes, all those human drops from the lush green of the woods!!! And there was no house that was not coloured red from the blood of its woman and did not cry unto Heaven. The caelum on my finger portended a red night for me! And I fell down before the Fakir, kissed his cold foot, and begged him to touch me too with his fleshless hand. It slowly drooped toward my shoulder, I did not even sense its musty scent, dying away as it fell. But contemptuously he turned away from me; I was unworthy of his pious works.

'Muktagirân!' 'Silika Unu geivuh …' 'Gadivatin' 'bivila yati hi!!!'

THE KHEDIVE

As Tino, the poetess of Arabia, begged entry before the portals of the palace, the concubines of the Khedive were sitting around the fountain in the antechamber and revelling in their intrigues. And when after some years' absence the white-bearded Mohammed Pasha travelled to the Nile capital for the festival of roses, as they went along the desert road his daughter Tino told of how she was mocked by the gatekeeper of the Khedive. That very night Mohammed Pasha woke his retinue. Sitting on his great elephant he rode over the reclining bodies of the dignitaries and slaves that they should not forget this hour. And they were to speak his commandments until the moon declined, and already it was turning in their mouths, a sacred dance. And when the great caravan entered the green city and the people in the streets asked the name of the princess with the shimmering eyes, they spoke according to the commandment of their master. But the Khedive's concubines had already drawn a bath for their guest and poured fragrant, poisonous oil in it.

And when they heard: Tino is dead – and the foreign princess, Pasha's brother's daughter, became aware of her friendship, they adorned her shoulders with chains and pendants and laid her down on a divan of silk; there she dreamed that her name had faded away like the call of the desert bird. And when the sparkling gold hand of morning laid its blessing on flourishing Cairo, she had forgotten her name, nor did any of those who had journeyed to Egypt with her and her father know it. But at story hour when she recounted the colours of singing soil to the young budding gardens below her window they were full.

But the great feasts began when the women attended once a year. The daughter of the white-bearded one sat beside the Khedive's heart and her lips murmured sweet songs … a shining band of love encircled his brow. And on the last day of the feast the Khedive raised the daughter of the white-bearded one to be his wife above all the women who abided in his love and in his palace. And whenever he enquired about the sweet murmurs from her lips, she hid her face in the lace of her veil. And her limbs glowed with the rushing colours of her thoughts. She was a volcano, withered from its own fire, a colourful spring that cannot tell of its burbling and drowns in its own spluttering. And the restless shadows of her soul filled the Khedive with sorrow, and to cheer her he gave her five hundred dancing dwarves as toys – and had them build a little town before her window. And he dispatched gardeners to her homeland to bring flowers from the shores of the Red Sea. He commanded that white horses and donkeys be brought from her father's stables, and the heavy elephant that had carried her and Mohammed Pasha to his land.

And as the Princess heard these joys of her homeland approaching, the neighing of her favourite horse, the shouts of the mischievous little donkey-drivers, and the heavy tramp of the elephant, she hurried toward the exquisite procession. And the Khedive gave a great feast; pipers and flute players filled the courtyards around the palace. The princes and princesses danced to their music, and everyone in the palace danced, even the goatherds. And the walls of the gardens began to turn, and the whole city danced to the bank of the river. And when the Khedive went to lead his dearest one to the dance, she was leaning against the back of the heavy elephant – Tino is dead! And the golden finger of the sun pointed to her name incised in the skin of the giant beast. – From the peaks of the pyramids the priests intone her tales every festival month of roses, and soon there is no one in the land who does not know them. But the merry locks of the Khedive hang rigidly around his face and all who behold him die from his pain …

MY LOVE LETTER

The stars peer blue through the golden sky, but the curtains of the harem windows are already drawn tight. The eunuch is wearing my black pearl earring on his thumb – and in return he calls us earlier to bed. The women are already dreaming of their new delicacies, of candied red roses; and slumber lies like doves on the cheeks of the little princes and princesses. And secretly I have escaped through the antechamber of the harem, the sumptuous doors of the great Sultan's hall close behind me, protective iron arms. And my devout friend awaits me, the slender candle on the marble table; she is ready to give up her life for me. – O Abdul, your eyes are ever roaming over the twilight, and my heart has turned blue, deep blue like the garden of the hereafter. I see you approaching on the crest of the Balkans, as on the hump of a dromedary. Abdul, I am in love with you, which is more intoxicating by far than if I were to love you. To be in love is like springtime … Great storms pass over my blood; I fear them, but I rejoice too in the shower of a thousand blossoming wonders. Too tempestuous were my thoughts of our reunion, and the veil before my face is rent. But the hour of our happiness must be mute, speak not, Abdul ... And keep your eyes closed, our love itself must not suspect that it is captured between our lips. The Great Prophet does not care for the infidels of your new homeland and their teachings, and he may be listening from a secret cleft in the night. But I have painted a dark star on my brow and it will all be nought but a seed unseen and our lips will remain buds, Abdul ....

THE MAGUS

The gates of enemy cities fell before Bor Ab Baloch's eyes and the Jewish commander, blessed of Jehovah, was felled by the jagged dagger of a thunderbolt. His son Abdul bears his harsh boyish eye sunk deep in his countenance, but his cheek smiles his mother's smile. Beneath the golden rose of the morning Abdul Antinous wanders along streams where the royal children are staring at their reflections. The Princess of Baghdad returns his gaze – her shading hand a golden velvet sail – Abdul Antinous …

All the suns sing before her soul, psalms that long for his iron blood scented by the smile of his cheek.

> Like dark jewels flows your slenderness.
> Oh my wild midnight sun,
> Kiss my heart, my red-pulsing earth.
>
> How wide open your eyes are –
> You have seen the sky
> So near, so low.

And on your shoulders
I have built my land –
Where are you?

As halting as your foot is the path –
My drops of blood become stars …
You, I love you, I love you.

THE GRAND MOGUL OF PHILIPPOPOLIS

The Grand Mogul of Philippopolis is sitting in the garden of the Imperial Palace in the Sultan's city when from out of the evening comes a foreign insect and stings him on the tip of his tongue. It is his habit to let it rest on his lower lip as he thinks. And while the physicians attach no greater import to the accident, it transpires that the illustrious master nevertheless imagines himself no longer able to speak. And he darkly refuses to entertain other means of making himself understood; the damage to the land is incalculable. Processions of flagellant priests move through the streets of Constantinople, and the Sultan is on his knees before Allah. He calls his two sons to his private chamber: 'Lads, you must learn a trade!'

Kings with sharp curved beaks have long threatened to devour the Balkans and it was only the skill of the Grand Mogul that protected the quarry. And from the roofs of the houses and public buildings, from the dome of the Great Mosque, boys call out their bulletins on the condition of the mute minister. –

My aunt shakes her head, she is sitting on her roof and her name is Diwagâtme. She was one of the thirty wives of my rich uncle, but he and her fellow concubines died of their wisdom; twenty-nine mummies around the grave of my uncle. I dwell with her because of her wondrous son Hassan, for I am a poetess. Every evening Hassan and I weep beneath the great stars – we cannot marry; Diwagâtme does not wish to build a palace for us. But she counsels me to weave a miraculous tale of consolation, for loosening the ensorcelled tongue of the Grand Mogul of Philippopolis is merely a matter of the right word. 'May his favour flow about you as a great stream of honey, my child.' And my clever aunt fills jugs with sinful Occidental liquid for the dry throats of the grim gatekeepers of the Imperial Palace. Wise men and physicians in foreign garments pace up and down between the pillars of the courtyards, tugging at their beards, deliberating and arguing with each other over the nasal cries of the donkeys in the stables. And undetected I reach the silent Grand Mogul; and I fold my arms and my veil trembles. But the illustrious master raises his red-bearded head closer to my conjuring lips, and his voice resounds louder than it ever did when he spoke. He pulls me down next to him on his tasselled cushion and he touches my cheeks, my eyes, my brow, and my veil is rent, and my breath is a mere flutter beneath his heavy pleasure. 'Now we are one state, one people!' he cries. But when the wise men and the physicians and the citizens from the streets and the Sultan borne on the shoulders of his runner storm the garden of the Imperial Palace, the Grand Mogul of Philippopolis lowers his head and is mute once more. But I am to confirm the report of his black servant. I am led into the Great Hall of the Imperial Palace where the official scribes record my invented, miraculous words, and the statesmen form a chorus around me, and the Sultan nods dismissively all the while and I am already quite weary of repeating my invented, miraculous consolation. And in a glass urn on blue velvet they bury the foreign insect from the evening, which I had boldly seized when it stung me on the tip of my tongue at the same hour as the Grand Mogul of Philippopolis, and robbed me of speech. 'And, oh Master, let me keep silence with you!' And I must dine with him from his golden bowl, drink from his goblet, and now they are making orange-yellow silk breeches and a cloak the colour of fire for me, such as the Grand Mogul of Philippopolis wears. And above us the trees are blossoming golden, and when the illustrious master slumbers, I think of the wondrous Hassan. But in the cool halls of the Imperial Palace, the legates await me. I am to secretly convey to them his opinion of their proposals having cleverly woven them into the conversation we conduct in the insect hour as we lay together. But the great many politically flavoured expressions make me forget the highly esteemed minister's responses, and from the parapet of the Imperial Palace in the company of the assembled company of august statesmen I present a garbled interpretation of the new taxation question concerning the levying of duties on spices from foreign lands. 'But the illustrious Master has often spoken vigorously in favour of the duty-free importation of nutmeg.' And already the illustrious master is ringing his bell, I am bound to his devotion. And an hour before the moon, the Sultan approaches to kiss the statesman's silent mouth, and he gives me rare gifts, and he has invented an order for me: the Miraculous Star with the Diamond. For the credit of the land has risen considerably, and the kings with the sharp curved beaks have swiftly taken flight, having acquainted themselves with our most valuable new projectiles. – But I have heard nothing more from the wondrous Hassan – I no longer take pleasure in the splendour all about, nor the honours bestowed upon me, and it amuses me to behold the baffled faces of the statesmen when I present them with the wisdom of my illustrious brother. The death sentence pronounced on the pack of stray dogs in the streets of Constantinople weighs on my heart – but I am looking forward to tomorrow's meeting in the Imperial Diet. Whatever the Grand Mogul of Philippopolis deigns to divulge is as sacred as the words of the Koran. And so they build dwellings in the Byzantine style for the neglected, howling creatures. The state pays Negroes and workers from the Occident for the construction of the buildings. And little palaces rise out of the capital's most valuable plots according to the plans of renowned architects. The Balkan inhabitants no longer doubt that blue blood flows through the veins of runaways. The faded canine aristocracy becomes fashionable, rich harem ladies spend thousands of piastres on shaggy dog princesses as playthings for their laps. And in every corner of the world they speak of the luxury of the Bosporus city, of its hidden gold fields and diamond mountains. – Twice each day, Ali Rasmâr kisses the mute mouth. But now I only speak in verse until the illustrious master has fallen into slumber. Eight hours long was his address on the drainage project, which he presented to me without a break. Oh wondrous Hassan … And above Constantinople the crescent moon shone with the first star as the wise men and the physicians and the citizens and the Sultan borne on the shoulders of his runner rushed to the garden of the Imperial Palace through cool rooms to the Great Hall – where the illustrious master has summoned them for his address. And I must confirm the report of the black servant, I have told the Grand Mogul of Philippopolis that I can speak once more. But his arched yellow eyes, which were just now shining unto Heaven in thanks, are bulging from their sockets, his red hair stands on end as though struck by wild lightning as he reads the bulletins of the Imperial Gazette. He silences the ministers with thunderous curses and they flee, and the Sultan hides behind the shoulders of his runner. Softly the tidings creep through the city of stars: the Grand Mogul of Philippopolis has turned raving mad. The robe is torn from my body, the veil from my face, my long locks cut off, and the angry Sultan has called a curse down upon me – and I am cast out of the garden of the Imperial Palace. Only one of the white donkeys from the stables follows me. Timidly I wander beside him through the night – across the square – there lives the wondrous Hassan but he does not recognise me, and he jeers at me, and from her roof my clever aunt Diwagâtme extends her hands in rejection. And an Occidental traveller comes and asks the price of a donkey ride on the shores of the

Bosporus. I have become a donkey driver, my shorn head is covered by an old fez which I found in the sand on the shore. And in the evening we lie beneath the great head of the moon, my donkey and I, and I divine my fate in the images incised in his hairy hide! ....

TINO TO APOLLYDES

For fifty-two moons Tino of Baghdad had not viewed the earth unveiled, and she grew weary of blind glances, and she cursed her long, brown hair and all else she had inherited from Eve. She wrote to Apollydes, a handsome Greek boy – he extolled love in the public squares of her city.

APOLLYDES AND TINO DREAM APPREHENSIVELY BENEATH THE DISC OF THE MOON

Calm light shines through the glass walls of the halls, and we are all alone in the glass castle, and our slender bodies are transparent, they are tender, and they sing. But a small, red drop of blood trickles on our temples, up and down, and spreads like a flowing circlet around our foreheads. We speak sonorous things, but our lips barely move, they are a secret colour, and our eyes are the sweetness of quivering summer nights. We know not what land we are in, it is hot, and in the distance black fires rise up, shining deep in dazzling roses. Our hands barely touch, but when the drop of blood rises in our temples our lips press against each other, yet they do not kiss, they threaten to burst in the wish to do so. At night we lie on white carpets and dream of cruel colours – or lustful figures come and toy with our tender, cool bodies as though we were dead infants. But our locks are singed by the glow of the little drop of blood, and our lips are open and they ache. The leaves in the gardens hum, and on the edges of the ponds are strange beasts, entrails, bluish, grey, ashen, and they keep nodding with their tongues; we stand on the glass tower of the castle and await the morning winds, merely swaying now, the silk of our robes trembling – our hands wish to touch, our lips to kiss, and our eyes are tense like stormy air. The glass walls of the halls convulse – we are searching for something – two cool, sharp pairs of eyes aim at our hearts – glass daggers they are, we see them again and again through fading mirrors – they have golden handles, delicate hands – they move, they wave to us – we wish to kiss … kiss! They wave – in our temples the drop of blood harkens, it reaches out its chalice to the infinite …

APOLLYDES AND TINO ARRIVE IN A CRUMBLING CITY

And when we awoke, a great finger stood in the sky, pointing out the way we should go. And we came to a crumbling city shaded by the head of a palm tree as old as Allah. And the old gatekeepers laughed when we asked the name of the city, and the elephant-skinned city piper tootled and pulled comical ghostly faces. '*Chabâah! Bâah*!!' But the maidens of the crumbling city accord themselves the queenly names of their mummies and bear the scent of the sacred river; they all dance the same tireless dance in dusty rags, *chabâah … bâah* … only the eye in the middle of their bodies watches, engulfed in the roots of love …………

TINO AND APOLLYDES

'Now kiss me!' said Apollydes. 'I do not know how to kiss, for the rose goddess of Hellas was angry with my father for his sacrifices to the Amazon.' I was astonished, and said, 'None ever spoke so finely of love as you, and yet you cannot kiss?' And I hesitated to kiss him. He replied: 'My lips are dreaming always of your fluttering dove mouth' …………

IN THE GARDEN OF AMRI MBILLRE

And as it turned dark, we sat on the silken flowerbed in the garden of Amri Mbillre, the King of the nameless city. Then my eyes, full of golden tears, began to sing love songs as we kissed. Amri Mbillre was wandering toward the moon; like the sleeping paths of the garden his feet floated around the silken flowerbed of our love. I warned Apollydes's open lips – but they were already calling to him. The King bound the Greek boy to a pillar in his palace and revelled in his flourishing pain. I will consecrate my crown to the vengeful love goddess of Hellas, to propitiate her, for on the public squares of my homeland where the handsome Greek boy extolled love the astrologers gather, but no one knows where he is, no one knows the name of the nameless crumbling city; my fearful breath has scattered the sands of the pathway that leads there …………

THE SON OF LÎLAME

When Lîlame, the wife of the Grand Vizier was still carrying little Mêhmêd in her womb, it transpired that a band of jugglers with light blue flax wigs made mischief beneath her window. And when Mêhmêd was born there were two tiny pale blue woolly hairs curled up in the middle of his bald head. It is said that his mother Lîlame turned melancholy at this, and his father, the Grand Vizier, summoned all the barbers in the land to the palace, but as they gathered around his son's scalp and its pale blue tufts they were perplexed. And Mêhmêd turned bitter at the world as he first walked the streets of Constantinople with his governor. The rich and the poor clutched their fat and gaunt bellies in mirth. And some of them even turned violent and tugged at the tips of his light blue curls. But as Mêhmêd grew older, he found an inexplicable appeal in striding through the mirthful crowds. His curls of blue stood out boldly from the lemon hue of his turban. And every year came the day of the great beheading. That was when all who could not keep from mirth at the sight of him were invited to the wide forecourt of his palace. The son of the Grand Vizier would sit there in an iron chair, forcing his victims to disport themselves as improperly as they had before him on the streets of Constantinople. But the people would tremble in distress, and the children would howl, for on a bench lay curved butcher's knives like crescent moons, in every size, to fit every neck. But none of them was ever blooded, for Mêhmêd would bring the agony of the guilty to an end by sending them back to their homes before execution. And soon they regarded the Grand Vizier's son with shy glances. The merrymakers hid their faces when they saw him approaching from afar. And the old women who sold spices and herbs in the public squares even whispered of the miraculous power of his holy, pale blue hair. Yet Mêhmêd was bitter at the world. But because he loved it so much, he began to whiten his extraordinary hair with liquid lime. And as I saw him doing this one evening, I went to him in the garden where he was sitting on the edge of the reflective lake, and his head was like a particle of Heaven that had fallen into the little body of water. 'What is my dear cousin Mêhmêd doing?' And I prevented him from continuing with his plan, for in the glow of his pale blue hair I divined the will of Allah. 'Mêhmêd, you are a wise man and you are a fool, for you do not know it. And were you to have your father's black hair or the golden brown curls of Lîlame your mother, the same fate would have befallen you.' I pointed to the lake. 'Your brow is inscribed in gold, how should the ignorant interpret its words, and your eyes see into another world.' And that evening we put it to the test; he hid his pale blue hair deep in his turban and through my veil I saw quite clearly how passers-by nudged each other curiously and cramped in mirth at the sight of him. But after that Mêhmêd would just pace up and down before my barred harem window until I joined him in the garden. His pale blue curls were no longer cut according to the custom of the land, they had already reached his loins, and one night at the reflective lake he revealed to me that he was inspired by the deep awareness that he was indeed a wise man and greater than all his fellow men, greater than the moon and stars. And he could only explain his indisputable enlightenment by the fact that he was a twin of Allah. And no longer would he walk the streets of Constantinople, trampling the little piles of people, that was not equal to his wisdom. He summoned surveyors from different lands to determine the height of the granite pillars on which the roof of his palace rests. He entered into wagers, and of course he always won. After all he was considerably taller than the stone pillars. And the pyramids on the far side of the river he built himself from the building blocks of the harem children. And the mighty mosque cupola was a mere dot beside his head. And his father, the Grand Vizier, took delight in the merry humour of his otherwise brooding son; his jests were even better than the jugglers leaping before the palace. But every day I grew more melancholy, like Lîlame, his mother. And it was early in the morning, the priests had not yet uttered their prayers when I heard Mêhmêd's voice before my window; he was waving a newspaper triumphantly in the air like a victory banner. And he barely allowed me enough time to read the great news. It concerned a monstrous great elephant from eastern India. At that moment it was in the imperial city of the Germans, in the Occident. – Twenty-five black servants and twenty-five servants of his colour were to ready themselves for the journey, as well as the highest-ranking men of the palace, and I, his cousin, who had first recognised his wisdom. On the voyage across the waters, Mêhmêd conducted himself in conspicuous silence, only now and then would a triumphant smile rise as fleet as leagues across his face and transfigure his pale blue hair. – Fenced in by three iron bars we saw Goliathofoles, the giant monster, with elephants in other cages shaking their heads as they beheld their neighbour. It was about to slurp down two barrels of water. On petition, the capital had made available the great drum of the gasworks for the esteemed guest – and the west of the city was cast into darkness. Goliathofoles was so tall – diligently one must report that snow lay on its head. But nevertheless it knew how to turn the organ with his trunk, and especially to beat the drum. Today, however, it resolutely refused to offer its tricks to the public, despite the numerous sugar loaves standing in readiness as reward. Mêhmêd's slender limbs clenched with impatience, and the twenty-five black servants and twenty-five servants of his colour harnessed their full strength to thwart their master's intention of entering the cage. He whistled cooing sounds through pursed lips, he tried to encourage the unruly giant animal. He threw biscuit crumbs into its cavernous open mouth.

He crouched ever smaller so that Goliathofoles could hear the encouraging drum roll of his hands on the buttocks of one of his servants. 'Good chiiild, good chiiild…!'

The people of the foreign capital had never before entertained such a delightful prince. But my heart ran with painful tears …………

THE POET OF IRSAHAB

Methuselah was nine hundred and sixty-nine years old when he died. At midday he was still out in the great marketplace in Irsahab, his fingers, the twigs of his long branch arms drooping down, and his mossy head bowing mournfully toward the earth. And the boys and girls kissing in his snug hiding place and the children playing their games in his shade feared his dark humour. And then his son Grammaton came and consoled him. His youngest was the only child of his last, hundredth wife who had been curious enough to marry this man as old as Heaven. And so it happened that Grammaton peered through blue eyes, for Methuselah was closer to the blue expanse than the earth. And Methuselah said to his son Grammaton, 'I shall die this day, for I cannot continue living without Mellkabe, my nurse.' Mellkabe had been buried that morning, and her lullabies were still lulling Methuselah to sleep from her grave. And he heard all manner of flattering names and Methuselah dropped down into the grave beside her. And an old raven sat on the edge of his plot, his name was Enoch and he was Methuselah's father. Following a dark transmigration of souls he had finally been born again in raven form, for he had insulted Vishnu, god of the neighbouring people. And besides him, the man as old as Heaven left three sons and an innumerable brood of children's children. And the two eldest sons were twins and five hundred years old, and Grammaton, his later offspring who bore so much heavenly goodness in his face, was born at the same time as the new constellation Pegasus. And Grammaton was a poet, and that was his misfortune for he could not distinguish two from three, and he had never had anything to do with the purchase and sale of his father's lands and livestock. And it occurred to him, when his five-hundred-year-old brothers explained it, that their father's legacy could well be divided into two, but not three, and Grammaton renounced his claim with noble tears in his blue eyes. But since then his grandfather in raven form had not left him in peace. He would set down on his shoulder, on the dreaming locks of his head, and once Grammaton heard him speak in a warning tone while never suspecting how closely he was related to the bird. Yet black suspicions grimly kindled his heart until his soul arose in the morning light and filled with gold. And he thought, I can only form my golden thoughts in stars and signs in the pillar that bears the roof of my father's house. But his shrewd brothers scolded him for his secretive ways, accused him of trying to take possession of their property, and he was cast out of Father Methuselah's opulent garden. And as the pillar that bore the roof of his father's house was the temple of his art, he began to hate his brothers, and he could not wait for the day when one killed the other, as Cain did Abel.

And his hatred extended to the children and grandchildren, and he scattered sickly seed among them, and they tore each other from the ground. But just as quickly they grew again, from children's children's child, to children's children's children's child, and when a father died a son would replace him in the night. And Grammaton saw that the whole city was kin to him, and his hatred grew from limb to limb and he trampled the wanton baby goat that stood in his path – lest it once again return on future stars as the son of the son of the son of some grandnephew to come. And he succeeded in rooting out the house of Methuselah, and that was all the inhabitants of the city, and not even its temple did he spare, nor the pillar that bore the roof of his father's house. And only the raven who could no longer die crouched in the hollow of his shoulders and he, Grammaton, sat on the tail of a stone monkey and sang:

> *i! ü! hiii è!!*
> *i! ü! hiii è!!*

THE SIX CHANGES OF RAIMENT

Six changes of raiment, spun from silk of dreams, rustle on golden hangers in the glass cabinets of my bedchamber. I am the Princess of Baghdad and in the time of the Great Moon I walk around secret fountains in bright rose gardens. The blossoming moon and star exude their scent amid cloudy black – I lay down to slumber in their lap ....

THE PRINCE OF THEBES

THE SHEIK

For my dear mother

So often did my father tell me this story from my great-grandfather's life that I now believe I lived through it myself ... Not even the insect repeller behind his great ostrich fan was permitted to overhear the discussion that my great-grandfather, the Sheik, conducted every evening with his friend, the Jewish Sultan Mschattre-Zimt. From the Jewish Sultan's simple roof a cloud led over to the inviting roof of my great-grandfather the Sheik, the High Priest of All Mosques. Often the Sheik was so impatient to see his friend that he forgot to say his evening prayer. The Sultan would cross the heavenly bridge; never too late, never too early. They would play enti. The balls would roll through narrow channels and drop into the chutes of the golden game; or it might be won with an accomplished toss after setting down in the first, second or third circle of the board. Getting the ball to stay in the third circle required great good fortune, so when it happened the whole palace knew of it. My great-grandfather's surprise would find expression in laughter (if he were the winner, that is) which shook the walls of the halls beneath them. When the moon rose, two Sudanese Negroes would bring beverages and the customary pipes to the two royal friends. The Sheik would smoke undiluted opium to increasingly severe rebukes from Mschattre-Zimt, worried for the damage the poison was doing to his friend's body.

Mschattre-Zimt possessed a collection which, in addition to the blocks of the tablets from Mount Sinai, included one of the Books of Moses, a scientific medical work in ancient Hebrew script. It was to this work that he owed his medical knowledge, which however he only exercised in extreme cases. For the Jewish Sultan was not a charitable individual. And even when he spoke of his friend the Sheik he expressed himself with the utmost indifference, but only out of an excess of caution.

My great-grandfather had twenty-three sons, including a pair of twins. The youngest of the twenty-three sons was my grandfather and his name was Schû. He was a chronicler and he would secretly sit at the entrance to the roof; in signs and stars he would record for posterity what the two bearded men said to each other. Whether Allah or Jehovah is the sole God of the world – this became the disputatious amen of their evening. Like the balls of the golden game, their words and gestures would come tumbling out in a rush. The normally dignified Sheik would forget himself to the point of throwing the pitchers of beverages over the battlements of his roof like an unruly boy until he wept with exhaustion. But Mschattre-Zimt would stand upright on my grandfather's roof, a shy smile in his big, brown eyes. The Jewish Sultan would leave the roof before midnight with a silence which made my great-grandfather ponder the waning of the darkness with sorrow. And when Schû, spurred on by his father, surprised the Jewish Sultan at the first ablution of the morning, it was not uncommon for him to swear never to visit his father again; but secretly he thought: in all of Baghdad there is not a Jewish servant whom Jehovah could look upon with greater pleasure than the Muslim Priest of All Mosques. For secretly, Mschattre-Zimt admired his friend's unbridled zeal. – On one of the feast days of the Jews my great-grandfather, the Sheik, the High Priest of All Mosques, rent his garments and cast ash over his glistening hair … Mschattre-Zimt had died that morning. The Sheik walked behind the simple coffin surrounded by his twenty-three sons; his friend was laid to rest like the poorest of the community in accordance with the justice of his laws. The Sheik said twenty-three prayers and one more, twenty-three at the grave of the Jewish Sultan for the number of his sons and one in Hebrew in honour of his friend. Then he fell silent, his face as mournful as the sky in the rainy season. And Schû, the youngest of his twenty-three sons, sat at his father's side, guarding his lip as though it were a locked portal. – – It was one year after Mschattre-Zimt's death that a mysterious knocking was suddenly to be heard from the palace wall. My great-grandfather was at the dining table with his twenty-three sons. The black servants who had gone to admit the guest found no one beseeching entry; still the knocking would not stop – yet they kept returning with the same message. Then Babel, the eldest of the twenty-three sons, went as well, but he too returned without the late arrival who was disturbing his father's rest. And each of the twenty-three sons went one after the other, searching the palace, destroying the dense leaves of the bushes, and lurking at the garden wall like bloodhounds. But the Sheik, my great-grandfather, donned his change of raiment and had his feet anointed with oil from the Tigris. His sons followed him into the subterranean vaults of the city; but the royal mummies were sleeping. And the priests in the mosques, suspecting nothing, made their sacrifices and consecrated their night to Allah. And they bowed to the Sheik and kissed his hallowed feet. A wailing wind was blowing through the streets of Baghdad from the direction of the Jewish cemetery; but when the father asked his sons to follow him there, they refused. He impelled them. For the gatekeeper of the cemetery was a sleeper and my great-grandfather's twenty-three sons had to form a ladder from the outer wall and down to the foot of the inner cemetery wall and the Sheik entered the quiet garden over the living steps of his sons Babel, Mohammed, Ingwer, Bey, Nessel, Hassan, Bôr, Abdul, Hafid, Schâl, Neu, Ismaël, Yildiz, Amre, Säuel, Nachod, Asra, Gyl and Gabel, Abel, Bab, Haman and Schû. Mschattre-Zimt had risen from his grave, the turban of Moses wrapped around his delicately twinkling brow – and his hand was raised just as he used to raise it to his God, as a sign of faith whenever he departed from his friend in anger before midnight. His diffident brown eyes were protruding from their sockets, weathered domes, cracked synagogues. The Sheik's body was seized by shuddering. In appeasement he placed his friend back in his grave.

The likenesses of my great-grandfather, the Sheik, the High Priest of All Mosques, and his friend, the Jewish Sultan Mschattre-Zimt, are carved into the gates of Baghdad.

CHANDRAGUPTA

For my son Paul

Chandragupta is seventy years old. His son will slay him in the early morning. Such is the custom of his house. And the women wail before their tents and their sons clap their hands in a transport of ecstasy. The new chieftain bites through the neck of an elephant calf, jumps three times over its upright stump – a chief to his people, for he bears the roof of his king. And Chandragupta, son of the slain, aged Chandragupta, loves the Melech's daughter. She lures him across the seas. And on a day of prayer for the people of Jehovah, the young chieftain secretly takes his wife away to his heathen land. And the Melech's daughter gives him a son, whom Chandragupta names Chandragupta, and Melech after his wife's father. And Chandragupta, the renegade son, yearns to be among the Jews. The heathen maidens love him, and one of them offers him her feather robe. Past every star he flies to the Jews. And the people of Jericho believe that an angel is at their gate and carry the sleeping man aloft on their hands into the city.

They go to the house of the High Priest and take him to the hill where the temple of Jehovah stands. For they have laid the holy stranger down upon soft moss beneath the balsam bush, and the daughter of the High Priest is washing his feet with water from the spring. Then the wind parts the stranger's feathers – he awakens – and the people see that this is no messenger from God, and they mock him. But a sage strikes fear into the disappointed crowd – that there is Shaitan. The High Priest takes the scorned guest into his house. The guest yearns to be among the Jews, gives gifts to the men in the squares and settles their quarrels and thus does he win the hearts of the Jews. And he helps the women pick roses. It is only Schlôme, the daughter of the house where he is staying, whom he never sees, and yet it is she who goes earliest to the bushes. And Chandragupta carves incense bowls out of elephant ivory for the altar of Jehovah. But the High Priest gently shuns them. This makes Chandragupta sad and so too Schlôme, the only child of the High Priest. And she begs her father not to spurn the pious gift from his guest; but the venerable servant of Jehovah turns his face away. Thereupon Chandragupta goes and chops the stalks of the black roses to build an altar to Jehovah, but the High Priest bitterly repels him. Now the son of Chandragupta the Chieftain weeps and Schlôme, the only daughter of the faithful servant of Jehovah, secretly sobs into her veils. And she scolds her father for his pride. At twilight she climbs the hill upon which stands the temple of God, unveils her face and loosens her hair, like Eve before her Creator, and begins to cajole her God, reminding Him of the pain of love when He was still named Sabaoth and that blind woman in paradise deceived Him, and her prayers become caresses, and thus does the only child of the High Priest transgress. She descends the hill and stumbles upon her house guest who is sitting beneath the balsam tree and yearning for the Jews. Limbs have leapt from the limbs of his limbs, which are longingly enlaced like the many-armed idols of his homeland. Ever since Chandragupta arrived in the city, grotesque old women have been secretly hawking forbidden playthings to the gentle maidens of Jericho on street corners and in the ditches behind their houses. Schlôme's companions keep the little pagan love gods imprisoned in urns and sleep with them as strange smiles play on their faces. But Chandragupta is seeking to win the hard-hearted heart of the priest. Laboriously he digs for gold in the woods of the oasis and through his labours covers the hill on which stands the temple of God for which he yearns. He embosses his living neck from the most precious coin of the Land of the Jews and places the breathing gold beside that which is extinguished. And from their roofs the people of the city see the shining hill; rush into the High Priest's house: 'The sun has fallen from the sky!' But he knows who has sown all that splendour and he hides his face; for he is fond of the stranger. And Schlôme hangs at her father's lap and asks him to grant the youth's pious wish. But impatiently he chooses two from among his honest shepherds to go to the hill that they might collect the gold in sacks so that not a grain of it is mislaid. Yet the living coin of golden flesh and blood has already gone missing. Then the sage knocks at the door of the solicitous priest and warns him that the people are offended; the grandson of the Melech will slay your only child, he tells him. But the sanguine priest reminds him of the morning when he cursed the gentle heathen of his house and frighted the people. They swarm in the squares in murmuring droves and gather before the house of their High Priest. The men pull at its firm roots and the women leap like cats about its beams. And they demand that he bring the peaceable stranger to Jehovah; insult their High Priest for stealing Jehovah' gifts. And Schlôme is standing on the roof; the city sees her bare face for the first time. Her voice sighs like a panting flame which stirs the people against her father. Chandragupta listens at the portal of his venerable chamber; his eyes are sunken and his breath hungers. Then he is overcome by that fever which afflicts his house following a lost battle. The stranger roams past the walls of the houses with his throat wide open. The cowed roses flutter on their hedges, his breath lashes the trees and the bushes. He sets about the raging crowd – 'Who would dare to subjugate Shaitan!' The trembling shepherds wade home up to their knees followed by their lambs, which are flecked with human sap. The evil star that is Chandragupta circles the hill upon which the temple stands, black blood seeping from his pores. And the people remember the sage and crawl on their knees, on their bellies they crawl over the roofs and force their way into the High Priest's house; demand his sacrifice, he who has brought so much ill-fortune unto the prosperous city. And Schlôme, hearing the sage's warning, anoints her limbs as though it were her wedding day. And like a delicate cloud she bears down from the top of her house, and wanders ever closer to the kiss of death, smiling all the while. The stars turn as dark as the Chieftain's head which so often menaced her from the veil of the sacred implements. Schlôme's sacred sweetness flows like rose-tinted honey over the names of the savage forefathers marked in pagan signs and figures on Chandragupta's flesh, over his golden loins. Rapturously he carries her body, his last sacrifice, over Jericho. The flattering darkness tongues the streets and squares, the fountains bleed no more. And Chandragupta emerges from the High Priest's house in Schlôme's veils like a woman of the city. Oh, so tender and tentative he is, like a woman heavy with child. And he sits among the shivering women behind the bars of the temple, his prayers sounding between his lips, the gentle cooing of a dove. There is nobody to impede the transformation of the Melech's grandson. Not even the servant as old as the temple in his greying change of raiment.

THE DERVISH

For Franz Marc and Mareia

The English ladies ride their donkeys along the hot avenue of tombs every evening; the sacred cats peer from behind the bars of the tombs and look worldly enough. The dervish is dancing. The ladies with the light-coloured eyes – ah, just like spring! – cease their chirruping, but the blue veils tremble on their hats. Every day my heart grows leaner in my chest, like the half-moon in the clouds. The delicate necks of the Western women rise from the hems of their diaphanous garments which hold their bodies as though they were standing in vases of glass. But I am wearing Yusuf's shepherd's cloak, dripping with lamb's blood just as his brothers brought it to their father. And I put the young dromedaries and camels out to graze and give them water from the wells. And in the evening, as the dervish dances before the cracked little mosque, I give the young humped beasts my dates and figs to stop them crying out for me. No son or daughter of the city has ever looked the dervish in the eye, the princesses of Cairo secretly wait before the dark sun of his lashes. All the golden images kissed the mosque for it birthed the dervish. I give him refreshment in the chalice of the dervish lily and blow the swirling sand toward Ismael-Hamed, who is leaning against the oasis thorn and who has lost the afterlife. In a sedan chair the priests' boys carry the exhausted priest, foaming, into his house. The English ladies ride their donkeys down the hot avenue of tombs, past the shining-eyed bars, on towards colourful prayerful night. Precious carpets consecrated to Allah drop from the roofs of the houses down to the stones of the street and await the red feet of the feast day of Yom Ashura. On the tenth of the month of Muharram it stirs the blood of the city to preserve the grandson of Mohammed, who was killed at Karbala that day. I chase my dromedaries into a column and my camels form a caravan. Men are already leaping through the streets in great bounds, their shoulders shaking up and down like the earthen jugs at the well. Christian dogs flee under a hail of stones, the bloodshed is anathema to the Jews. Noble Arabs, statesmen, priests in embroidered saddles pass by on arrogant horses. Countless bodies launch themselves beneath countless hooves. My lips are already black with blood. The incense of blood seeps from the pores of the city. The women crowd at the open harem windows. Sickle eyes, almond-gold, cinnamon-coloured, swarms of shimmering Nile eyes hover over the deathly procession. The young holy men lash themselves with whips, others whet weapons on the columns of their spines. Daringly the English ladies lean over the railing of the roof casting half-blossomed buds of nightveil and nightshade upon the dervish. He is riding a camel, drunk on Allah and bearing the white dove of Mohammed, the light of the afterlife, on the golden bough of his ringed finger. I cry out. The dervish waves. A noble young Mohammedan launches himself beneath his pious gait; but I climb the rear hump of his beast and hold on to its tail as it threatens to stumble over crushed corpses. At times the dervish gently turns his golden brow towards mine. His fine nostrils are of gold. My limbs hold their breath and listen to melodies; there is a palace on the Tigris that belongs to my father and my mother, who have been slumbering in the vault for seven years. My mother's hands are two embalmed stars, and the beard of the white-bearded Pasha has descended, a silver curtain over proud ancestors. And I exchanged the princess's veil for the shabby cloak of the field. Ismael-Hamed is now tying up the young pack animals. I explain: 'Abba his long-haired camel is buck-nosed, and Rebb tosses my fez off my head with his tail, and my she-camel loves Amm, a dromedary from Ismael-Hamed's herd.' The smiling dervish bends his upper torso this way and that: night and day – the glittering pearl tassels of the royal saddle sound over Bedouin hands as if they were brown carpet fringes. Our beast sinks into a pool of blood, it drips warm from my face, these are living raindrops, the time of consecrating Heaven nears; Allah is watering the world with his nectar. But Ismael-Hamed will not see the fragrant wonders which will grow, he keeps his head bowed. Slender boys vie for the quick path to the sparkling afterlife, but our camel chooses not to trot over their famished bodies. The children's calls drown out the wild prayers of the half-priests. The flat nose of a single-humped beast is already sniffing at me and its throat presses impatiently at my back. The dervish signals for the little beggars to move away. 'Lord, why do you bar the gates of the golden garden to them? And yet you know that their fathers rebel against the Koran. Shall they atone like Ismael-Hamed the shepherd? Instead of the light he carries the dark image of his vanquished infidel father in his breast and so poor is he that he is ashamed to cast his eyes upon me. Behind your pious beauty I thought I dreamt a blissful reason to seek a hereafter for him here in the damask of this sumptuous procession. Lord, forgive me this evil thought, I hoped that one of the consecrated might lose his salvation before the darkening threshold of death!' The alarmed dervish fumbles pensively in the direction of the ragged children. They are building their lives up, head upon head, playing pyramids. Over the back of the beast I lean out over the expanse of blood, but I am seized by the eyelashes of the priest; the shadow of his empty eye sockets cast across the bleeding city. His pious father, who pricked out his round lights, rests in Allah. Red we wade through the bright spray of red. We ride through a painting. The Nile is painted red. I beat my brow on the hard pillars of the houses; I am in darkness, my eyes are frozen. In the horror of its secret tombs I lose my afterlife; it has fallen into the lap of Ismael-Hamed the shepherd. He bathes my frozen feet in the warm milk of a she-camel, but my face is already leaning into the wind. Blossoms bloom; onto its banks the Nile washes up the rotting bodies draped in folds of water, their souls departed to the beyond. I recognise the three Bedouins by their slenderness and the noble

Mohammedan by his girdle. The ragged playful children were trampled by a dancing horse's hoof; they have no more little hands for the begging. – Above Cairo floats the prayerful glow of the Koran.

A LETTER FROM MY COUSIN SCHALÔME

In the harbour of Constantinople lie golden boats – stars …. I am in the palace of my great uncle; we cousins from Baghdad share a scent of old walls, we princesses from the Tigris dance with silent limbs. And I do not understand the tongue of the women in the harem. I know not what gives them joy, what causes them to quarrel. They speak not their Sultan's tongue; 'we speak Parisian,' the youngest explains to me; her hair is red – 'chic'. At times she hums skipping songs. I hunger, I float above the colourful mosaics on the floors; I fear the evil dishes and beverages which are secretly smuggled into the women's chambers. They eat forbidden meats and we drink red and yellow murmuring beverages, our heads rocking all the while. And I am ashamed in the presence of the eunuch, his eyes bulge, the sick old man. When I think of our eunuch – his cheeks are round manna cakes and his voice warbles merrily like a jester's flute. I wish I were back in Baghdad. Here the finest cushion is reserved for the eunuch. My aunt and her daughters are on their knees in a wreath of bright colours around him, they all wear wide trousers and my old aunt's are wider still and made of floral brocade. Their laughter and their exposed gestures bore me, I wish to bathe but I am ashamed to lift the veil from my face before the toadying voice of the eunuch. My possessed aunt in her oversized brocade trousers begins to disrobe; curious, the other women follow the eunuch's instruction. On the carpet he opens a large book with horrible pictures. His voice loops a lustful brook about the feverish wits of the women. Behind the curtain, beneath the dove of Mohammed, gentle guardian of the harem, are sharp, jagged racks, whips and pitch torches. This evening my aunts and cousins have forgotten me entirely; I know only that they scream through my dreams like mothers torn to pieces by their dead children. I tremble, the eunuch reaches for one of the many whips; each strap has lead shot at its tip; he whets it side to side through the air several times then slowly lowers it to dash against the wide, full moon of my feverish aunt's behind and she, I swear to Allah, turns it towards him wherever he moves, screaming blue murder, coquettishly baring her teeth at him. Her daughters are seated on the divan; enviously they bare their breasts which bloom in speckled gold carnations. The eunuch draws sharp little needles from behind the curtain. I creep across the carpet out of the women's chamber on all fours and stand behind the window in the antechamber. I long to board one of the little celestial messengers on the Bosporus – the sky is one great star.

THE FAKIR

For the Prince of Moscow
Senna Hoy, unforgotten

The three favourite daughters of the Emir of Afghanistan are named Schalôme, Singâle, Lilâme. Their faces are like milk; slaves shoo the sun from the women's roof as if it were a bothersome bird. The Emir's three daughters stroll beneath tamarisks and mulberry trees of an evening, or to pass the time they are carried in carved sedan chairs past the gold bazaars; the Emir could do with rich sons-in-law. He is my mother's cousin, but this is the first time I have been invited to his court. We dreamers from Baghdad have always been a bad influence on the daughters of foreign palaces. My great uncle says we drag a bad star behind us, and his noble daughters reject the glass baubles I have brought for them. But I know how to gain vengeance. 'Where is your uncle, Schalômesingâlelilâme?' For they are ashamed of his squalor; he leaves a mark on the milky white neck of their mother, the Emir's wife. In secret the old slave woman informs her that the Fakir is back at the court; can she hear her brother warbling? Out of his sack of snakes crawls a young viper, smearing slime around his sullied chest. But Singâle casts a queen's droplet, a noble little piece of gold stamped with her mother's head, into the shoe that her begging uncle has pulled from his suppurating foot. Singâle likes to tease her mother, she has inherited her Old Syrian nose which once even taunted one of the Jewish tribes. Snuffled scraps of food are set before the droning Fakir in an earthenware dogs' bowl. Sometimes when he is sated he sleeps between the pillars of the harem courtyard on his living sack of serpents which rear up to form a mound, only to sink back to pliant length under the burden of the sleeping man. Schalôme stands at the window in the moonlight framed by a round golden backdrop. And her sisters, summoned sleepwalkers, fall back into their pillows. The scent that seeps from the pores of the Fakir awakens the blood, like throbbing berries, the drink forbidden by the Koran. It torments the youths' intestines and the daughters of the city secretly sip at his scent; their bodies blossom like brown and yellow roses. Lilâme, the second daughter of the Emir of Afghanistan, has been carrying a breathing toy in her womb for moons, today the Turkish prince forgot his turban beneath the arbor vitae in the women's garden. And Singâle loves Hascha-Nid, who is the son of the Khan, the white-beard of a wild tribe; his skin shimmers in sundry sweet colours. But his garments are austere, he has entirely neglected to put on jewellery, as is usually the custom at war dances and the ceremonies of their idolatrous rites. Ever since Singâle pointed him out to me I have not closed my eyes. They keep staring across the sugar fields in the direction of the wild martial chants. And as I was painting my face, in the mirror I saw the Fakir and I took fright; he was sitting on the wall of the courtyard, kissing his snakes. There was one that yielded wildly to him; he stuck it halfway down his grey, crawling mouth. Ever since then I anxiously watch out for the three sisters during the night that they are not startled by my braying. Sometimes Schalôme cries out; Lilâme flirts with her pillow which is silver like the prince's turban. And Singâle looks enviously at my lips, which are parted in spasms. I hear the howling of the wild warrior women – Hascha-Nid, the son of the Khan, is dying. The Fakir coils along the evening paths of smiling plants; he is to perform a miracle on the white-beard's son. Schalôme stands at the window in the moonlight, she gently strokes my hair, the wind tears it from her hands and waves it over the sweet fields. I wish to kiss her hands, but a drop of blood from my evening's repast still stains my lips. I keep waiting among the tall reeds, keep his limbs hidden in my jaws, and soon Schalôme shall be wed; a caravan of Indian elephants approaches bearing gifts for her, and on the leviathan's trunk sits her crowned betrothed who will bring her to his house. 'Schalôme, what dreams do you have of him in the night?' 'My uncle's snakes always come and strangle my dream.' And when Lilâme sees her uncle, she hides her white paradise, now blossomed, beneath the arbor vitae in fear. Only Singâle's cloudy silk lifts away from her white curves, but the dying chieftain's son shuns her speckled pink carnations. I am no longer allowed to sleep in the same chamber as Schalôme, Singâle, Lilâme; my great-aunt, the wife of the Emir, heard my roar of joy. Schalôme's gentle hands tremble, everything she holds drops to the carpet, she has St. Vitus' dance. Every evening the Fakir warbles in the courtyard. Schalôme's expressions dance to his notes. Draped only in the cobwebs of the old walls, I wander the earthen vaults of the palace. It is from there, Singâle tells me, that her prince will escape. And I have drawn a glowing streak down my chin, my mirror warbling wedding music all the while. I am also wearing the long gold earrings that Schalôme gave me. The sisters say I have a golden body and they wish to lure out the shy sun once more. Hascha-Nid has a golden body too, if we were to cross we would be a golden palm tree. I am weary, I should like to be buried like the degenerate uncle is several times a year. The father of the worms yearns to return to his earth. Then the wife of the Emir exhales to the far end of the riverbank, and her breath halts the whisper of young lips and casts sobriety over the sons and daughters of the city. I stumble over raised earth and reach into a waiting grave. Upon the upturned covering of earth lie small, shining implements which serve to detach the membrane that connects the tongue with the lower jaw. I have seen them doing it in the mirror: they stuck it in his maw like a plug to stop his breath. So sadly I hum; Schalôme crawls into the grave after him. And no more will she find me. The streak down my chin runs through my whole body, cleaving it in two. Is Hascha-Nid dead? I hear the wild women rampaging as though possessed, their voices multiplying horribly in the overwrought reverberation of the vault. I wish my father were here, I would float back into the palace on his long beard and into Schalôme's lap, which sways like a dancing serpent. And her restless, gentle hands would creep across the dust of the floors. There is a warbling in our chamber with the four silk cushions, filled with the Fakir's alluring muskroot. Schalôme rose an hour before midnight and she smiles once more in the moonlight. Then the old slave woman saw her dash down the last steps of the harem staircase. I cut open my veins with my glass baubles. The palace is deaf and dumb, Lilâme and Singâle are two ancient idols. The Emir of Afghanistan orders all the ramparts in the districts of the city dug up. Corpses lay bare of their earthen shrouds on the slabs of the cemetery. The air is chilling. The divers scoop beneath the waters of the river. At times the Emir casts an enquiring glance at me. We maidens from Baghdad drag an evil star behind us; yet I shall not betray Schalôme; and I wish my father were here, his long beard blowing careless melodies out of alley maws and away from the city. Heavy-hearted, I think of her in her dark waiting palace … Schalôme crawls into the grave after him.

THE BOOK OF THE THREE ABIGAILS
ABIGAIL THE FIRST

For Venus, Kete Parsenow

He was still in his mother's womb when he became Melech. The Melech's mother lamented because Abigail refused to be born. He lay secure in his mother's sumptuous womb and snored so loudly that his slumber could be heard from the palace right across the river, all the way to the east of the city. The young Melech did not wish to be born. And Diwagâtme, his mother, outgrew the King's cushion, and a room in the palace was upholstered for her great womb, and there she spread out day by day. The young Melech had now been dwelling in her womb for twenty years and refused to be born. The Melech's mother then summoned one man from each group in the city to advise her. The most distinguished priest of the Jehovanites, one of the cattle breeders from both the red and yellow Adamites, and the dearest of the boys of Sabaoth who was to have been the playmate of her son Abigail. And the market square was hollowed out and padded with soft sheep fleece for Diwagâtme, for with her body in this state the mother of the stubborn

Abigail could no longer stay in the palace, and so one midday it transpired, on the counsel of her medical advisor, that innumerable slave hands carefully carried her to her new position in the middle of the market square in Thebes accompanied by music from bagpipes and bells and drums. Abigail refused to be born. But one day his mother heard him utter a heavenly melody and it made her think of the Song of Songs of Solomon, yet she kept this new secret of her body from the city and even from those closest to her. Her son Abigail was no ruler but a poet; while she understood his desire to stay in that dark, untroubled night, to others it was an ever-expanding mystery. But the burden of this secret made Diwagâtme ill; shadows shrouded her shining eyes, and she became dumb with fear that one day she would weave her son's poetic soul into an indifferent conversation, especially as her only joy was to hear her son's Song of Songs. Nor did she wish to be touched by that little polity that formed around her body like an island, inspecting and taking measurements. The persistent Melech, however, kept living off the flesh and blood of his mother, and she felt most distinctly that he had a fondness for certain dishes, that he only versified when he enjoyed the sweet blood that came from his mother eating candied roses. But whenever the impatient citizens of the city approached his mother, he crept deep into his lonely, pounding home until that day when he kicked his mother's heart into her ribs with great force and killed Diwagâtme. Then the matricide refused no more – to be born out of frozen night. Diwagâtme was buried, but he, her son, was set upon the throne in the palace. Abigail the First sat naked on the throne in his last skin, which was tender and new and pristine. And out in the wide world he was afraid – his hands kept searching for walls and the daylight hurt his eyes. But his citizens carried him on their shoulders throughout the city, throughout the land – their miraculous Melech! Abigail was handsome, each of his limbs rested; every tint in its proper place! All the daughters of Thebes were devoted to him; the long expectation in which the city had lived had left them with imploring eyes and parted, smiling lips, and in their hair they wore flowers with an open chalice for the butterflies. Yet Abigail crawled into the belly of every virgin and now longed only for the moon when it pounded round and tender in the sky. Then, early one morning, his palace caught fire, killing Abigail the First, the son of Diwagâtme who took to her grave the secret that her son was a poet. He stood and took a step and for the first time walked on his own two feet, the feet of a spoiled King which had otherwise reclined on the shoulders of his citizens. The palace was ablaze by the time Abigail noticed, whereupon he climbed down a column of the building, collapsed in a faint, and was trampled by a caravan still dreaming in the dawn. This was the end of Abigail the Late-Born of Thebes.

ABIGAIL THE SECOND

For Karl Kraus, the Cardinal

Abigail the Late-Born's eldest cousin Simonis sat on the throne of Thebes for just one day, got bored and renounced the crown in favour of his brother Arion-Ichtiosaur. The brother called himself Abigail the Second, in memory – as he professed – of his late-born predecessor cousin. This second was almost nothing like the first. For the new Melech was sixty years old when he ascended the throne of the city; his original nature had taken on a burnished form, benevolent, serene and solid. He ascended the throne on the tenth of the month of Yisroel and kept his dreaming people awake and alert. He invited the oldest citizens of the upper city to his palace and granted them a silent address of nods and gestures, wrinkled his illustrious brow a few times, seized the tenderest of the wealthy merchants, kissed him with a force which made the man, so distinguished in the eyes of all his fellow citizens, cry out, amazing and delighting him in equal measure, along with the other astonished onlookers. Then the little group was mutely dismissed with a most gracious smile from their Melech. They took the well-tended paths and scattered beyond the gates of the palace garden, through the crumbling streets, smiling sheepishly. When pressed by the curious crowd, they were only able to shrug their shoulders and secretly explain the behaviour of their new Melech to each other as a sign of grace; they bowed their old heads in their turbans and did their strange king's bidding. He recruited men, most of them over-fed until they were as round as balls, to preach abstemiousness in the market squares in the name of their concerned Melech, and several times a month they forbade the spoiled populace from enjoying fruit, bread, fish or any form of meat until not a dish was left and the people went hungry throughout the day. But the Melech permitted any citizen of the city of Thebes to witness his own meal, to delight at the melons at his table. And he sowed hatred, greed and envy among the gentle people such that they would begrudge themselves a date. Then one day his favourite slave asked him: Lord, why do you command so? To which the Melech replied: hatred and greed and envy keep the people alert. Abigail the Second had the Tropic of the Monkey tattooed on his cheek; he studied astronomy and mathematics, and his work chambers were hung with charts of these sciences. Abigail the Second had his laughing women and his weeping women; as well as this band he was accompanied by his Greeter, a noble youth of amiable form who courteously relieved the Melech of the exertion of greeting each passer-by. At his side, however, was his Explainer, whose role was to interpret the zest of the jests that were presented for his high spirits. Every citizen of the city was permitted to approach the Melech unhindered, on the street or in the palace, with an anecdote; often he would take a leisurely evening stroll in the refreshing air. Or he would stand on the roof of his palace and argue with God. Or he would teach his servants and handmaids the story of Creation. As he was childless, he adopted the two dead sons of Adam and Eve; never did he believe that Cain committed the bloody fraternal deed. He had the son of the High Priest paint the brothers on the wall of his banquet hall. Yusuf, the son of the temple, who was intimately acquainted with the palace, once witnessed a dialogue that the Melech held with his red domestic creature, Bisam-Ö. He had advised the highly troubled king to wed. This adviser felt that the grumbling he had sensed slowly growing among his people, especially among the youth, was linked to the absence of an heir to the throne. Abigail had devoted himself to his beloved citizens with the entirety of his exalted person, and he was pained by these hushed agitations. He had endeavoured to stir the lax people of his city, he had tried to get each and every one of them to stand on their own two feet, which is why at the beginning of his reign he began breaking up all the associations that had formed under Abigail the First. Only the Sabaoth boys, the youngest citizens of Thebes, continued to hold their secret gatherings in defiance of the Melech's prohibition, led by the gifted son of the High Priest. Yusuf raised himself up from among his youthful followers to be their prince. One of the Sabaoth boys, whose father had won the Melech's favour, was summoned to the palace by the King and gifted with all manner of jewellery, nose studs, golden belt straps and chains, but on pain of observing the custom of visiting the Melech several times each moon and kissing the sacred toe of his foot in deepest gratitude. This act, which the inexperienced boys found humiliating, kindled their anger to a pillar of fire which strode before them. Yusuf, the son of the High Priest, loved the young Queen Maryam, the chosen bride of his hated Melech, and his heart was envenomed with envy at his old crowned rival. Once as young children they had met behind their city's hedge of love and loved each other. The land of Maryam, the High Priest told his son at the time, has a fragrance of bread – –. The boys discussed among themselves how they might prevent the Melech's wedding, until they stumbled upon a plan which enlightened and inspired them. Their Prince Yusuf had long enraptured the weeping women and the laughing women and he persuaded them, the poor idlers, to carry out the deed. The laughing women began hanging their red hearts mournfully on the clouds and the laughter of the weeping women turned the day lunatic. But the Melech was already making preparations for the arrival of his young bride. He had had two baboons trained and they sat among his servants at the entrance to his palace. The sun tumbled brightly over their ugliness and the orange of their rear ends dashed about with their impetuous leaps. Then the Queen arrived. Abigail's Greeter and the Melech himself conduct all manner of polite formalities between his laughing women and weeping women, his leathery brow tenderly rouged, his beard dyed a young man's shade. 'Look upon Abigail, our Melech!' With dancing steps he advanced towards his joy. And several of the Sabaoth boys were hiding behind the laughing and weeping women and they tickled the weeping women on the hips until they began to laugh at the welcoming ceremony, causing utmost embarrassment to the Melech. Maryam the young Queen was cool and self-seeking and ambitious. To please her royal host she had enriched her mind with the lustiest anecdotes from every land. The flute players played dance melodies and the bagpipes distended like mirthful bellies. And when Maryam told the Melech her anecdotes to the accompaniment of the music, the laughing women began to sob so forcefully that the food on the table floated away on their tears. But the Queen was most profoundly struck when, as she spoke from the depths of her heart, the weeping women began to puff and burst with laughter, confusing the King, who was not at all versed in the sentiments of woman but who finally, trusting in the response of his slaves, loosed a flood of laughter himself, forcing a smile from the Queen which shimmered as bloody as a garnet on the raging ocean. After the feast, the Melech led his high-born bride through the crowd of guests, but with a gracious nod of her grave, haughty head the piqued Queen left the astonished court, the city of Abigail the Wondrous who, as its citizens related, had died because his Explainer failed to explain the meaning of the strange anecdotes at the feast. In reality, however, that same night Yusuf, the son of the High Priest, had killed him with a dagger to the belly. Yusuf, the Prince of Thebes, had his small army of a thousand Sabaoth boys proclaim him King Abigail the Third; together they summoned the city's citizens, who exhaled with relief.

ABIGAIL THE THIRD

For Professor Walter Otto the great youth

The former Sabaoth boy Yusuf, the son of the late High Priest and his beautiful mother Singa, was now Melech in Thebes. In addition to his royal duties he held the highest office in the temple. His seventeen-year-old face and his limbs were in bloom, and his heart was an oleander bush. His mother Singa, who as a virgin had shared with her friends an affectionate fancy for the late-born Melech, stoked her son's hatred of the second Abigail into action. He who had kept the city sleepless, weary and frustrated now at last lay in the vault and slumbered. Thebes inhaled deeply in its festive garments at the wedding the Melech celebrated with the city. Neighbouring towns dispatched magnificent gifts to establish friendly relations with him and his court; Prince Marc ben Ruben of Cana extended the bond of brotherhood to the seventeen-year-old. He gifted him horses beyond compare for his stables, sacred cows and calves and long-haired goats for his groves. Among the many guests who paid their respects to the King from throughout the world was an amiable old Sioux Indian who was a passionate admirer of the first Jewish Melech, Saul. Abigail the Third enjoyed chatting with the copper-coloured man about the people of the Ark of the Covenant; he also discovered in his foreign friend a great skill for producing dyes which he deftly extracted from the bark of various trees and colourful herbs. And there were portraits in Abigail the Third's hand which made landmarks of his courtyards for all time. But in front of his palace he created the stone image of his mother Singa. Abigail surrounded himself with harpists to sweeten the feasting hours; and dancers meandered over the mosaic blossoms on the floors – it was not uncommon for them to have their veins pricked and to proffer bowls with libations of their red berries to their dear master. And Abigail the Melech built magnificent palaces and places of worship and served his young god Sabaoth. One day he said to his boys: 'I should like to see "Him" or even just His finger shining in the moonlight.' And he anointed six of the wild Jews as chieftains and gave them royal names. To one of them of whom he was particularly fond he gave a new name of unexampled tenderness. Salomein wore a star at his temple and he was immortalised in a carpet to the right of his Melech. This beloved playmate loved the King for as long as he lived. And Abigail and his chieftains entered the houses of the old citizens who still held to the strange laws of the second ruler; they forced the fathers to surrender their captive sons. And twenty-five thousand youths went into holy battle for the territory of Eden under their Melech's command. At twilight, treacherous women crept into the warriors' weary tents hawking the resin of love from the forbidden tree. Just as Abigail the Third crossed the waters of the Pishon with his rapturous army and claimed victory east of the river, riots broke out in the noble quarters of his city, but Singa, the Melech's mother, succeeded in assuaging the anger of the parents who had been robbed of their sons. The joyful victory march was preceded by a great number of captive heathens; Abigail ordered their veiled goddess to be borne to the temple on the shoulders of his war slaves. He forgot that he was offending God with this cult. But the Sabaoth boys built a golden wall of their shining bodies around their Melech and guarded his breath, and listened to the words of his talking dreams, and they enriched their tongue such that any foreigner who heard the Sabaoth boys converse could scarce withstand the beauty of their speech. Sometimes Abigail's companions saw him climbing the hill of the city alone or accompanied by his favourite Salomein or by his host of chieftains. When the comet was among the stars he would not be drawn from the summit, a golden bird. But once he wept so wildly that his tears fell upon the fields of Thebes and they were made fruitful. He was often to be found behind the brightly coloured bread flowers exchanging pious oaths of love with Salomein. Or he would sit in his love chamber and blow kisses to his citizens. In the transport of his love he would climb the pyramid in the city square, tear the silk from his chest and bleed for his people like a young lion. And although it was forbidden by law there was not a house in Thebes that did not adorn their portrait of the Melech with a starry cloak, a warrior's helmet. A wealthy Jew had him set into the wall framed by lapis lazuli. Among the Occidental enemies near his city, Abigail the Lover saw blond hair and blue eyes for the first time. From his roof he admired the fair locks of the sleeping men and failed to come to the aid of friendly tribes when they were attacked. When he awoke from his blond rapture he sentenced himself and signed his own death warrant. But the Sabaoth boys turned to the Balkans and the Sultan, who was impressed with the royal warrior's sense of justice, annulled the valiant death sentence by inviting the Melech to his court and giving him the hand of his daughter Leila. But when the blond foe besieged the gate of Thebes to seize the old city and kindled the King's heart anew, it transpired that as the Sabaoth boys were measuring the depths and breadths of the river, Abigail approached them in precious jewels of war, a shell girdle around his loins – the companions cried out in surprise: 'Oh, look how the war adorns our Melech's face!' – he then demonstrated his fine spear throwing for them as though he were preparing for a festival. Hiding behind a sheaf as his warriors exchanged blood with their foe, Salomein saw – how the two splendid rulers of the enemy armies lovingly embraced one another. But the news that the Melech had forced the foe to retreat without bloodshed rushed throughout Thebes, and from that moment on he enjoyed a respect from his people which extended to his closest companions, and even Salomein was moved by tenderness to respectfully touch his fingertips with his lips, his eyes shyly avoiding the wistful smile of his royal companion. And so Abigail the Lover became a lonely prince, achingly recollecting the nights when he wrapped himself in the skins of sweet bodies. Returning home from a walk, he saw the companions who had been scared away, playing at the edge of a lemon grove with the princesses of Thebes, and Leila, his wife, was among them; she ran to greet him and anxiously handed him the roses from their game. To be so misjudged filled the loving king with a deathly thirst. He fell upon the Sabaoth boys' cuckoo and ate the heart from its breast. But the loyal, confused youths threw dice to choose who among them should take the gruesome act upon himself for their King. The fateful number fell upon his favourite. When Abigail heard that his Salomein was dead he fell into a wild faint. At night he would stand before the gate and threaten his guiltless city. Or he would wallow in his own blood, and in war he became the most dreaded foe. Wounded on a tiger hunt, he died early one morning without regaining consciousness. The Sabaoth boys demanded the Melech's mother hand over their companion; from his bones they created a temple.

———————

SINGA, THE MOTHER OF THE DEAD MELECH THE THIRD

For Erik-Ernst Schwabach and his wife

Singa, the mother of the dead Melech, sat in her chamber wrapped like a mummy, and for three years the people mourned with her. Then one day she tore the cheerless veil from her face to hear the hot psalm of love which was churning up the dirt of all the roads, muffling the roar of the river, creeping into the hearts of the people and revealing their secrets. Agitated, the Sabaoth boys then went to the Melech's mother in the palace; their faces bore the features of her son, and in all of Thebes there was not a princess whose mouth had not transformed into the Melech's delicate lips. And Singa herself was astonished to discover that her hands resembled the toys that Abigail used to play with on her lap when he was little. And the slave women smiled at Abigail's mother in that peculiar way her own fair darling smiled. Anyone who let a distracting sound slip from his lips was stoned, for the Melech's mother sent her black servants, who were skilled in listening, to seek the source of the magic psalm; they brought no answer; a merchant woman who sold cloths and glass beads to the maidservants in the lower chambers of the palace sought admission to see Mother Singa but she was refused. But she hid behind a nutmeg bush and cried out in the darkness: 'Melech Mother, Melech Mother, my son is a cattlehand and he has an ear that reaches to his loins!' He pressed it to every wall of every house until it was worn out and no bigger than those of the servants in the palace. And he knew from whence the yearning song came. Then the mother of the loving Abigail the Third summoned all the noble daughters of the city to the palace and chose the most gracious among them to be wed to the royal temple. But the bride hanged herself before the gruesome wedding. And none of the other daughters of the city would enter the temple, so Singa offered her jewellery to any dancer or prostitute who would take this walk of love, besieged the huts of the poorest shepherdesses and kissed the maids. In the field the ears of wheat began to burn, and the vines in the vineyards, and the hearts of the people of Thebes crumbled to ashes and the winged figures on the fountains in the gardens flew away. And Singa, the Melech's mother, had her cheeks rouged like a maiden and her lips painted for a night of love, and she wore gold rings on her toes and fragrance in her hair, and all the people stood around the temple until she emerged, dishevelled; her limbs were eaten away, the rags of her maidenly garments hung about her, and tears ran from her crumpled eyes. Since then, all the citizens of the city have crept along the pathways as though they were going to the cemetery and their dwelling places have become as quiet as houses of God. So ends the story of the third Abigail, whose love claimed so many victims.

AN INCIDENT FROM THE LIFE OF ABIGAIL THE LOVER

A story of Mary of Nazareth
for the Venus child,
Kete Parsenow when she was five years old

When Abigail the Third was still a Sabaoth boy and filled with much yearning, he rode his white camel, accompanied by his playmate Salomein, through the places of Palestine and came to Nazareth. There the children of the rich and poor all sat together on the cracked stone steps of the city's playing stairs and sang a wondrous, sweet little song in Old Nazarene Hebrew. And Yusuf set the smallest of the children upon his great beast and had Salomein write the little verses from the child's babbling lips on a slate. It sounded like this:

Abba ta Maryam
Abba min Salihï.

Gad mâra aleiyâ
Assâma anadir –
Binassre va va.

Lala, Maryam

Schû gabinahû,
Melêchim hadû-ya.

Lahû Maryam
alkahane fi siyab.

Dreams, tarry, Mary maiden –
All about the rose wind
Snuffs out the black stars.

Cradle your little soul in your arms.

All the children come
Zotta hotta riding lambs
To see the Little Godlet –

And all the
shimmering flowers
on the hedges –
And the great sky there
in its short blue gown!

THE CRUSADER

For Hans Adalbert von Maltzahn
in commemoration

The Crusaders bring their peal to the city of Jerusalem and sin overgrows the proud Muslim blooms on the pathways. I pluck the petals of this sin where I find it, the secret buds of the Christian who invited me to visit his daughters in his garden. They have blue eyes and yellow hair and they say the snow too is yellow. And it shall snow in their garden, for it has trees with cool leaves; what was it the sisters called the flowers in the beds? The bells peal again as they do whenever new Crusaders march through the gate into the city. Fair they are and tall as towers. Their helmets bear the sign of the Cross. I am wearing the holy warrior's robe of my homeland, as I have ever since I came to the garden of the rich merchant in Jerusalem with a dagger in my belt, as curved and ineluctable as the sickle moon. The sisters says that this is the custom in their city. They have conceived a passion for me and they regret that I am not a prince; they scatter forget-me-nots on the path for the crusaders who do not see the heavenly little droplets;

but sometimes their eyes will strafe their angelic faces with valiant devotion. The two blue-eyed maidens sleep in beds at night and they laugh at me when I ask them what they are. A forget-me-not sky hangs above their beds - - - the next world is veiled from us. Were I one of the Christian's daughters I should give the Crusader who advanced into the city that morning a bed of breathing wood as white as her skin, for he was freezing in the mild early sun. Ever since he looked over the fence into the garden, I've been threatening myself with my glittering sickle and reaping the sweet gold of my heart. I know his name, the sisters read it over his shoulder in his church book – his script is tall and slanted – I follow the infidels into the church. Since then, the arches of the mosques have dampened my erected dreams. There are now ten thousand Christians in Jerusalem who wish to exterminate sin – – so great it cannot be. And the merchant's daughters embroider crosses on delicate bands of love which sprout like the smooth pathways of secrecy. But with triumphant smiles the Crusaders kiss the cross work stitched by angels' hands. I never see him among the recipients; yet he seeks my mouth beneath the morning star. My cousin Ichneumon of Uskub now wears the holy warrior's robe from my homeland, but his arms tremble for love and cannot withstand the foe. His entire army roars like a heart, like my heart, and they are all delivered unto the Christian dogs. I am lying beneath the canopy of the two sisters, I have the Oriental thistle; spikes pierce my limbs and the most merciless of them penetrates my heart. Angels, the two of them – – cast a blue gaze over my face and battle with the dove of Mohammed who wishes to tear my veil to shreds. But I cannot stand the goodly angels for they are Christians. And yet secretly I climb over the garden fence into the church nave at night. There on the balcony sits the knight in his long ceremonial tunic playing chorales on the organ; the dying sounds are a balm for the dead. 'Knight, the Kings of Sinai made mourning women howl for their dead, and the festivities of their harps turned the lips of old men crimson and unborn boys beat at portals of body's gold. When I began dancing to your chorale before the church altar, my body slumped; a grim disc of a moon, which just now had been the most playful star of them all.' Then snow fell on the knight's cheeks and I saw that the snow was white, not the colour of the sisters' hair. They always stand at the fence with their dyed snow hair, bestowing sweet piety on the Crusaders. And they wish to prepare a bed of breathing wood for them, as smooth as their skin. But you, knight, you shall sleep upon a dancing star in the night! And with great effort I climb over the fence of the garden, a small thistle bush grows from my toe. And in Baghdad the war rages. The desert is a shield to our warriors. But my cousin loses every battle. The city's sacred garment is a turncoat, its warrior's robe is devoted to the foe. Half-recovered, I am borne to my homeland, Baghdad, to answer for the holy garment. My father caresses my hands, my fingers like weary rays. But a lust for battle blinds my eyes. Ichneumon of Uskub is already standing before our palace. I pull the last splinter of thistle from my toe – – *abbarebbi, lachayare, lachayare!* Passionate martial music bears me aloft on its shoulders through the streets. That very same night I vanquish the Christian dogs. My father tends my courage and my valour like two grandchildren. Never before has a Princess of Baghdad advanced into battle. Only my cousin's snivelling lip droops; he says he strung himself up in the lemon grove forest but is unable to find the tree again in the morning. When the moon is round we plan to advance on Jerusalem. But the elder warriors in the war building do not agree with the notes of my strategy. Their minds became entangled on the battle plan; but the Grand Vizier instructs them: Allah's spirit has come upon me. – Sometimes I feel that my gaze is blue and I flee my father's face. In my eye the young Emperor Conradin stands in his helmet and cross. But every day my father checks my armaments and the ankles of my camel; he has grown old. Ismael-Hamed, the Grand Vizier's son, will keep him company while we drive the interlopers out of the capital. He knows how to pander to his peculiarities. And my father wishes me to wed Ismael-Hamed before the great battle. But I tell my venerable Pasha that the number of mummies in his young friend's vault is not meet for a Princess of Baghdad. My handmaid had a dream that I was sitting in Ismael-Hamed-Morderchei's splendid sedan chair, dressed for a wedding, and Ismael-Hamed his son was lying in the vault. The Grand Vizier managed to bear my struggling soul on his shoulder, but my kisses closed before the late summer. He gave me the most peculiar gifts: a ring with a stone which reflected Mount Sinai and earrings which held a tiny clock in their pendants which rings every two hours for prayer. And two albino Negroes to accompany me into battle that I should not lapse into melancholy. Whenever those four white-eyed eyeballs with the red dots stare at me, I laugh so hard my camel's hump wobbles. *Abbarebbi, abbarebbi, lachayare!* My mount carries me over the farthest gorges, trots ahead of the army over lush paths in the early morning light, riding red the length of lips. We can already see the gates of the city. My warriors fall to the ground and mumble verses from the Koran. How I hate that plain tower of the cross! The pious Muslims from Mecca and Medina, the peoples of Yemen and Tyre, the Bedouins, the inhabitants of Nineveh and the other lands of the Euphrates, the Egyptians, the Philistines, the Edomites, Amonites, Hittites, the tribes of the Jews: Chaldeans, Saduccees, Judaeans, the great-grandsons of David, the sons of the Levites and their fathers, the high priests of Jehovah, Talmud scholars from Damascus – they all stand with me against Christendom. I look out over my proud army, *abbarebbi, lachayare - - - - - -* even Ismael-Hamed-Morderchei follows my troop - - - *Lachayare!*

The two rich merchant's daughters throw themselves at the feet of my camel and entreat me in the name of Christ. Their forget-me-not canopies bleed like the wounds of the knights. A battle breaks out beyond the hills of the city. We penetrate the irksome churches of the infidels. My warriors and I smash the altars and sanctuaries; Ichneumon of Uskub impales the young Emperor's squire on the top of the cross tower; I have my cousin's turban removed as punishment for his brutality. At night I dream hidden behind the knight's eyelashes; I heard him play chorales as his houses of God were dying, and tirelessly I stood with my back against the little door of the balcony, behind which he sat in his long ceremonial tunic. I kissed his knees, I, the Princess of Baghdad – – – my kisses left bloody marks. So gently I cry, I, Allah's warrior; I lay my hand on dead words to swear an oath. Ismael-Hamed-Morderchei enters my splendid tent, he is dressed in European garments like the gentlemen of the delegations in our city; he strokes his pondering brow, a polite chill arises between him and the speaker. His beard is not a cloud like my father's; stones like noble potions shine through the parting in his chin hair. With a well-groomed gesture he accepts from my hand the letter from the young Emperor Conradin, who is suing for peace. His two emissaries stand clasping each other in astonishment. They hold me to be a figure from A Thousand and One Nights. It pleases the Grand Vizier to stoke their fancy. He points out the twinkling of my brow, and my hands which are images of the moon yet can cast a spear. I am surprised by the mockery with which he hurries through the royal letter, I cannot believe that the curly-locked messengers have been bribed by my cousin, but the Grand Vizier then surrenders them to the enemy as is the Western custom. Perhaps by evening they will be dead. Ichneumon of Uskub is absent, indisposed. The foe's sword broke in two against his wilful buttocks; but through the screaming of the shed blood I hear his calls and I miss my stark-staring frights; they love him, for amusement he lets them leap over his arm like two dogs. He knows that without them I cannot penetrate the heart of the Emperor. He approaches among the foremost ranks of the enemy. The holy warrior's robe envelops me like a suffocating sun, my arms begin to dry out, and my breath fumes in the eyes of my warriors …

My face opens out over late dancing bodies and temples as nothing before. My two Negroes trill their shrill war cry whenever my spear pierces a knight's chest. The Grand Vizier drives the jesters before my camel, they beat hard, numbing music with their teeth and dance to it: *Abbarebbi, abbarebbi, abbarebbi, abbarebbi, lachayare! Hu hu u u u u u u u u u*

    When Conradin the young knight and Emperor was buried, his mother came on a pilgrimage to Jerusalem, and when she met my Negroes, she laughed at the unnatural sight. I kissed her robe - - *abbarebbi, lachayare, lachayare .... abbarebbi!!*

AFTERWORD

In the last summer of the 19th century, two incidents in the life of Else Lasker-Schüler signalled the vivid if perilous existence she would pursue in the century to come. In July 1899 her poetry first appeared in print, the following month she gave birth to her son Paul – whose father was not her physician husband. Together these events made it impossible for her to persist with the illusion of genteel bourgeois domesticity she had fitfully maintained to that point.

Thirty years earlier she had been born as Elisabeth Schüler to an assimilated upper middle-class Jewish family in Elberfeld, now part of Wuppertal, the same dense industrial Rhineland conurbation which first inspired Friedrich Engels's investigations of capital and labour. Else, as she was universally known, stood out even as a child for her dark brown eyes, bright red dresses and precocious literacy. She experienced anti-semitism at school but retained largely happy memories of her childhood, along with her *Plattdeutsch* dialect.

At home her brother Paul would tell her the story of Joseph and his brothers, which she would in turn act out for her mother. The figure of Joseph became a reference point of profound and persistent identification. It bound her to the memories of her two most cherished family members, whose deaths – at the threshold of her adolescence and her majority, respectively – were devastating events in her early life.

In 1894 Else Schüler married physician and chess master Berthold Lasker, twinned his name with her own and moved with him to Berlin. The capital offered welcome opportunities to pursue her growing interest in art, and Dr Lasker provided his wife with a studio as well as lessons from artist Simson Goldberg, who introduced Lasker-Schüler to an unconventional side to Berlin previously concealed to her. By 1899 she had also evidently met the arch-bohemian writer Peter Hille, although surprisingly for such a consequential encounter their first meeting is unrecorded. In any case it was apparently Hille who suggested that her primary calling may lie in writing rather than art. She could not, in view of this ragged, destitute, sunken-cheeked character of no fixed abode, have claimed ignorance of the sacrifices the creative life may demand.

And by 1899 Lasker-Schüler had certainly met the man who fathered her only child Paul, named for her brother. All her life she maintained silence about the father's identity, or put the curious off the scent with fantastical alibis. Yet she may in fact have identified him in her writing, as we shall see. But the recurring convergence of the fictional and actual throughout her career raises the question: to what extent can or should we examine Else Lasker-Schüler's prose as encrypted accounts of figures and events in her life? On the one hand you could certainly argue that her body of work deserves to be assessed on its own terms and not reduced to soap-operatic elements, regardless of correspondences with biographical data. But sometimes the parallels are too pressing to ignore, and a writer of the stature of Else Lasker-Schüler, you might counter, does not simply assign the attributes of associates to her characters arbitrarily, therefore these links merit investigation. Both approaches are equally and simultaneously valid, for in Lasker-Schüler we find a figure for whom the distinction between life and work was unusually fluid. And nowhere is this more apparent than in three interconnected texts which she published in the decade preceding World War One: *The Peter Hille Book*, *The Nights of Tino of Baghdad* and *The Prince of Thebes*.

Else Lasker-Schüler greeted the new century as a single mother in all but name, rarely more than a few hot meals from penury yet eager to embrace her freedom. It was a time of discovery and deprivation she would mythologise in *The Peter Hille Book*. The most important step in this new existence was her encounter with Berlin's utopian Neue Gemeinschaft (New Community), which she presumably found through the intercession of Hille. Both idealistic and hedonistic, the Neue Gemeinschaft initially convened in bourgeois Wilmersdorf before moving to a villa in lakeside Schlachtensee, outside the (then) city limits. Its packed agenda of revels offered a 'boat ride to Elysium' in Lasker-Schüler's words. As well as the brothers Heinrich and Julius Hart, who had been major voices of Naturalism, the Neue Gemeinschaft included anarchist writers Gustav Landauer and Erich Mühsam, the artist 'Fidus' (Hugo Höppener) and philosopher Martin Buber. But the three men to whom Lasker-Schüler was particularly drawn were Georg Lewin, Johannes Holzmann – and Peter Hille.

Born in Westphalia in 1854, Peter Hille issued just three novels and a drama during his lifetime; these and his posthumously published works are little read in German today and have never been translated into English. If Hille is remembered in his country of birth at all it is generally as an extreme example of writerly asceticism than as an actual writer. A school friend of the brothers Hart, as a young man Hille came into an inheritance which he squandered in the bohemian manner. He spent time in London, where he met Marx and Engels, before moving to the Netherlands where he gave the last of his money to a bankrupt theatre. In 1885 he sought to establish himself in Berlin, where he launched his own newspaper – which lasted two issues (two was also, coincidentally, the number of subscribers). Hille spent much of the ensuing decade in penniless vagabondage before trying his luck in Berlin again in 1895, lodging with friends or sleeping in parks. The years of indigence left their traces – Stefan Zweig met Hille towards the end of his life and estimated his age at 70; he was actually in his late forties.

Even among the struggling writers and artists of Berlin Peter Hille was a cause for concern but his apostolic charisma and aphoristic utterings drew a modest cult of young followers. There is no indication that his association with Lasker-Schüler was ever romantic but he served as a mentor and together they became the most notorious and uncompromising of Berlin's bohemians. Hille and Lasker-Schüler took part in readings and other activities of a Berlin group which had significant overlap with the Neue Gemeinschaft – Die Kommenden (The Up-and-Coming). A loose association in which the Harts were once again instrumental, it was led by Ludwig Jacobowski, who had published Lasker-Schüler's first verses. Unlike the Neue Gemeinschaft, in which Lasker-Schüler was the only woman of note, Die Kommenden had a significant female presence, hosting readings by the likes of Marie Madeleine, the Wilhelmine Sappho, and Dolorosa, the rhapsodist of masochism.

These groups were fired by an indeterminate religiosity and a Nietzschean quest for transformation, a syncretic longing they shared with many others in Germany at the time. They included Rudolf Steiner, who headed Die Kommenden after the death of Ludwig Jacobowski in 1900. Lasker-Schüler's sympathies for reformist ideas were finite – she was never a candidate for communal living, for instance – but she harboured a similar desire for freedom and expression, and began to explore alternative personae in writing, both poetry and prose. As she wrote, she wrote her new self – or selves. Her very name with its three rhyming pairs of syllables had rhythmic elan, but it was Hille who endowed her with the additional name 'Tino', an ambiguously gendered identity. In letters he addressed her as feminine

(Liebe Tino!), masculine *(Mein lieber hoher Kamerad!),* even neuter *(Liebes Tino!).* In 1900 she was already signing letters with this name or variations thereof ('Prince Onit') and in turn named her mentor 'Petrus', the first of the many guises she crafted for her associates.

The paths of Petrus and Tino now converged. When Lasker-Schüler submitted 'Sulamith' to the Jewish journal *Ost und West,* a verse in which she prophesied 'my soul is burning up in the evening colours of Jerusalem', the Catholic Hille responded by incorporating the titular biblical figure in his contribution to the same publication. And both of them saw promise in cabaret, a performance form which arrived in the city with the new century. Well before the Weimar era, Berlin rapidly developed a bold, sophisticated and surprisingly transgressive cabaret scene, and Hille and Lasker-Schüler were there from the outset. Witnesses to Lasker-Schüler's readings were particularly struck by her unabashed expression of desire. Along with Marie Madeleine and Dolorosa she was pressed into the category of 'erotic' poets – or 'poetesses of horizontal mysticism' in the impertinent description of René Schickele – late blooms of the hothouse flowers which had enraptured tremulous souls in the 1890s.

In 1901 Lasker-Schüler and Hille took part in two performances under the name 'Teloplasma', an ambitious format which combined text, artworks, décor, music and other elements to create something like an 'environment'. These events were organised by Georg Lewin, who was now going by the name Herwarth Walden at the suggestion of Lasker-Schüler, with whom he was newly romantically linked. The first evening was dedicated to the 'tragic', the second, a few weeks later, was 'erotic'; unsurprisingly, this was better subscribed. Lasker-Schüler's presentations for the 'erotic' evening were subject to censorship before she even made it to the stage. But on this occasion her humid poetry failed to win audience favour and overall the Teloplasma experiment was a critical and financial failure.

Else Lasker-Schüler issued her first volume of verse, *Styx,* in 1902 under the auspices of Berlin-based Danish publisher, Axel Juncker. Later that year Peter Hille launched his own cabaret, enlisting Lasker-Schüler, Erich Mühsam and other friends to appear at Dalbelli's, a canalside Italian restaurant popular with bohemians in the early 1900s. Proceedings were overseen by an image of Hille as a one-eyed Odin by artist Franz Stassen.

The following year Lasker-Schüler dissolved her marriage to Berthold Lasker and wed Herwarth Walden. She was almost ten years his senior, although throughout her adult life she freely exercised her prerogative to dial her age down by up to a dozen years. Walden, an ambitious, well-connected catalyst finely tuned to the changing oscillation of the time, was already marshalling the avant-garde forces that would form the Expressionist movement.

Both Hille and Lasker-Schüler contributed to a journal established in 1904, *Kampf.* Its publisher was their Neue Gemeinschaft colleague, the Jewish bohemian anarchist Johannes Holzmann who was now going by the name Senna Hoy, a phonetic reversal of his first name – another of Lasker-Schüler's inventions. Hille contributed a profile of Lasker-Schüler to *Kampf* which long served as the standard description of his acolyte:

Else Lasker-Schüler is the Jewish poet. Of great accomplishment. A Deborah! She has wings and fetters, the joy of the child, the pious fervour of the blessed bride, the weary blood of banished millennia and old slights. In dainty brown sandals she wanders into deserts, and the storms dust off her childish bibelots [..] The black swan of Israel, a Sappho whose world has been rent asunder. Shines like a child, is most dark. [..] But Else's soul stands, as she once so winningly put it, in the evening colours of Jerusalem. [...] A second volume of poetry is in print. See you soon, Tino! Tino is the impersonal name that I invented for the friend and the person ...

Ominously, a Lasker-Schüler short story entitled 'Der tote Knabe' (The Dead Boy) appeared in *Kampf* directly after a Hille piece on 7 May 1904. This was the day Hille – having collapsed on his way home from Dalbelli's – died, at the age of 49. The second book which Hille mentioned in his article was *Der siebente Tag* (The Seventh Day, 1905), in which Lasker-Schüler marked out even greater distance between herself and the conventional poets of the day, and which included perhaps her most celebrated verse, the pre-Expressionist 'Weltende'. She then turned to address the greatest creative influence on her life to that point.

In the beginning was the word, or in this case the name; *Name ist Programm,* as the German idiom has it. 'Name is no accident,' said Lasker-Schüler herself.

'Kabbalists were able to draw out the root of the name. So the name of each petitioner would be their reckoning, their summation, their extract.' Hille himself dwelt on these meanings: 'My name is Peter. That means rock,' as he wrote in an essay on religion. 'And a rock I wish to be, a solid, sentient rock that can feel reality, and God.' Her previous life wiped away like her footprints, Lasker-Schüler echoes these allusions to the Gospel of Matthew and awakens to her new existence only once Peter – or 'Petrus' – names her 'Tino'.

Thus begins *Das Peter Hille-Buch* (The Peter Hille Book) published by Axel Juncker in 1906. For Else Lasker-Schüler, this first book of prose was an undertaking of enormous significance. She referred to *The Peter Hille Book* as the 'foundation' of her life, her 'Bible' – a 'Bible that seeks not to convert' – or alternatively her 'blue Bible'. Blue carried intense meaning for Lasker-Schüler and it recurs throughout the book, not just in the expected skies and waters, but also gardens, fruits, silks, pennants and a language Tino shares with Petrus.

Else Lasker-Schüler's main goals in writing *The Peter Hille Book* were twofold. First, it was her memorial to Hille himself, one she claimed its subject had actually commissioned. 'Before he died it was the wish of the prophet: "Tino", that's what he called me, should write it. For me this was a prestigious wish which I fulfilled with great pride and good cheer. I walked with my holy manuscript, my blue Bible between my hands – an altar wherever I went. To immortalise the great writer saint with the earth that preserved him struck me as a worthy amen to our wanderings'. In the auto-referential way that characterised their interaction even after Hille's death, this 'commission' is included in the work itself ('You shall prepare a throne for my remembrance'). Saints are celebrated on the day of their death, and it is significant that here Lasker-Schüler locates Petrus's birthday in May, the month in which Hille died.

The second goal was to record the author's own development as an artist and newly liberated woman seeking fresh forms of existence in what was at once a rejection of the Wilhelmine mainstream and a pledge of commitment to her new principles. Much of *The Peter Hille Book* reflects Lasker-Schüler's revelries with the Neue Gemeinschaft, her search for independence, for companionship, for transcendence. While Tino is rarely the driver of the narrative, she has agency and assumes the role of apostle or apprentice normally reserved for men, and is at times taken to be a boy. Lasker-Schüler in fact referred to herself as the 'truest and youngest' as well as the 'most loyal and noble of [Hille's] disciples', using the noun in its masculine form.

The Peter Hille Book is a set of episodic miniatures, 47 in all, most of them just a single paragraph and more than two thirds of them containing the name 'Petrus' in their title. Like a transcription of the panels in an illuminated manuscript, the book presents near-allegorical figures in schematic environments. We follow the journey of Petrus and Tino, although this journey has neither a fixed destination nor a stated purpose, and it is one the two are happy to share with others at various points. Seasons, months and feast days are named, yet the historical epoch is unclear until Tino notes that she parted from Petrus in 1903. The unidentified settings read as Germanic – forests, lakes, fields and particularly mountains; Petrus and Tino are drawn again and again to the heights. This corresponds with notions of a return to nature circulating among the author's utopian friends at the time. The book begins with the protagonist's flight from the city and the narrative only returns to urban locations for brief intervals.

Lasker-Schüler's 'blue Bible' bears the influence of the actual Bible, although tellingly, the original renders much of the Joseph-like narrative of 'Petrus Puts a Farmer's Son Back in the Earth' in the *Plattdeutsch* dialect of her youth. There are also elements of Germanic and Nordic myth, of fairy tale and classicism, and parallels with Hille's own (then) unpublished work *Das Mysterium Jesu*. But looming even larger over *The Peter Hille Book* is Nietzsche. Its elevated, scriptural language is a direct inheritance and many contemporary readers would have recognised Petrus, seeking the eremitic isolation of mountain peaks, as a kindred spirit to the philosopher's Zarathustra. The impact of Nietzsche on the generation of progressive writers born around the beginning of the German Empire in 1871, who hungrily absorbed not just his radical philosophy but the sacramental clarity of his prose as well, cannot be overstated. Writer Paul Goldscheider records Lasker-Schüler as saying 'Friedrich Nietzsche created the language in which we all write'. He further claimed that Lasker-Schüler herself, as a young woman, had encountered Nietzsche in his final years of incapacitation when he was in the care of his sister Elisabeth. While this is not corroborated elsewhere, in the most overtly Nietzschean section, 'Petrus Puts My Passion to the Test', her Tino recoils at the cat crouched jealously on the prophet's tomb, whom we may imagine to represent Elisabeth.

Elsewhere in the book, direct associations between characters and figures in Lasker-Schüler's life can be made with a reasonable degree of certainty. In Antinous we have the sensitive young poet Peter Baum, another native of Elberfeld who sometimes shared the cabaret stage with her; Grimmer and Najade are his siblings Hugo and Julie. In real life Lasker-Schüler did at times leave her son Paul (Pull) with her sister, who appears along with her nieces Edda and Erika (Sage and Haidekraut). Goldwarth is readily identifiable as Herwarth Walden and the book thus serves, among other things, as an eccentric account of the couple's early courtship. Hellmüte is an unflattering stand-in for writer Martha Hellmuth, Sennulf is Lasker-Schüler's treasured companion Senna Hoy, while the chieftain Bugdahan is modelled on writer Samuel Lublinksi (who ironically commented after publication that *The Peter Hille Book* would be 'indecipherable' to future readers). Onit von Wetterwehe, meanwhile, is thought to be based on writer Gerhart Hauptmann. Readers who found Lasker-Schüler's cliquey myth-making to be an exasperating nonsense may have taken comfort in Hauptmann's 1910 novel *Der Narr in Christo Emanuel Quint* (The Fool in Christ Emanuel Quint), which offers stinging characterisations of 'Peter Hullenkamp' and 'Annette von Rhyn' (Hille and Lasker-Schüler):

> Peter Hullenkamp, with mattress feathers in
> his dishevelled hair and a long, kaftan-like cloak
> which he kept on because he was wearing it
> directly over his shirt, was in fact the figure of an
> apostle. [...] In reality he was a man out of time
> who formed a distant future and a distant past
> behind his steep, huge forehead in a perpetually
> fermenting fairy tale. And Annette von Rhyn,
> who went everywhere with him like Antigone at
> the side of blind Oedipus, was completely enclosed
> in this seething fairy tale through him, and he
> through her. She called him by turns a King of
> Taprobane, an Emperor of the Seven Floating Silver
> Islands, a Guardian of the Hanging Gardens of
> Semiramis. Four weeks long she called him the
> Duke of Ophir, for the next four weeks he was her
> Harun al Rashid, the Caliph, and she lived with
> him by searching for fleas at tables overloaded with
> fruit, spices and drinks in their palaces, served by
> the hundreds of slaves of their imagination.

Considering her status as a Jew, a woman, an artist, an impoverished bohemian and (mostly) single mother, it is significant that the characters she inhabited were generally of noble birth. Yet Lasker-Schüler was hardly ignorant of the conditions in which she lived or the contrast this presented to her high-born avatars; those illustrious titles often appeared at the end of begging letters. But asceticism itself, she infers, can elevate and ennoble. In 'Petrus and I at the Feast of Onit von Wetterwehe', it is Petrus's cloak, the signifier of his poverty which had so discomfited the royal guests, which raises him and Tino above their crowned heads.

Petrus presents as a character beyond development. Hille was not even dead before Lasker-Schüler began the process of canonising him – or petrifying him, a man who to her seemed 'hewn from stone'. Here, with her customary immoderation Lasker-Schüler compares her adored Petrus to Poseidon, Noah, even Satan. A recurring figure of identification is Odin, the one-eyed weather-maker, and the cover bore Stassen's portrait of Hille in this persona. Hille was notorious for scribbling on scraps of paper he kept stuffed in his pockets, and here Petrus takes his scroll out whenever inspiration strikes. But it is the life of the writer rather than its product that we witness – a preview of posterity.

Tino must find her own way in the world of words and early on she rejects a mouthpiece of literary convention who is proffering a 'large book, full of vain letters which formed rhymes'. Lasker-Schüler exercises her artistic liberty to the full in a prose analogue to the inventive language of *The Seventh Day*. *The Peter Hille Book* contains neologisms both allusive and elusive; to cite just one example – 'zweigereigeneige' is a carousel of a word containing two sets of three internal rhymes. Depending how you choose to break it down, it holds the German words for 'two', 'branch', 'round' (in the sense of dance) and 'incline'; it is offered here as 'twisting-twigling'. It was the kind of formulation which later attracted the indignation of antisemitic writer Ludwig Thoma, who equated this 'linguistic syphilis' with the presence of Jews in Germany. Even more enlightened readers may blanch at the periodic outbreaks of whimsy – lullabies, fairy tales, the sun anthropomorphised as a woman in a gold robe. But the sincerity of the acolyte's offering is beyond dispute. Peter Hille was the rock upon which Else Lasker-Schüler built her church – meaning her writing, her identity, her life. And even within this structure future developments are taking shape. The 'Oriental' elements in *The Peter Hille Book* – turbaned Jerusalemites, Petrus's Arabian journey, Tino's masquerade as Scheherazade – point the way ahead.

Even before *The Peter Hille Book* was published, Else Lasker-Schüler was penetrating further into her imagined East, and she presented the initial findings of her expedition in January 1906 at her first solo reading at the Architektenhaus, a key avant-garde venue in Berlin. *Die Nächte Tino von Bagdads* (The Nights of Tino of Baghdad) danced into existence in summer 1907, again published by Axel Juncker. In this loosely episodic work we again see through the eyes of Tino, but she is now a 'poetess of Arabia', a 'Princess of Baghdad'. In an indeterminate period and time scale we accompany her through various named sites along with locations either unnamed or invented which can be collectively encompassed by the term 'Orient' in its archaic sense. Befitting a princess, Tino associates with important personages: moguls, caliphs and khedives, some of them her relations – her father the Pasha, her uncle the Sultan of Morocco.

In the 1919 edition of the book (the basis for the translation presented here), along with the relatively minor changes to the text one might expect after more than a decade, the most significant amendment was the removal of almost all of the verse that had featured throughout the first edition, leaving only a few lines at the end of 'The Magus'. Most of these nine poems had been published in other venues in the intervening years, and their excision lends the work greater cohesion. The slightly amended title – *Die Nächte der Tino von Bagdad* – emphasises the feminine identity of the titular character.

Like the protagonist, the book appears to arise in dance and assume form through movement, its ethereal opening passages cohering into something more corporeal. A brief yet insightful early review by Hans Bethge referred to it as a series of 'dithyrambic prose sketches', capturing this key motif of dance, both sensual and ritualistic, as well as the abandon and irregularity of the book's form and its ecstatic, Dionysian quality. The disjointed style also reflects the fragmentation and abrupt shifts of early cinema. The constituent parts range in length from the few lines of 'The Six Changes of Raiment' to the episodic 'Grand Mogul of Philippopolis' and encompass elements of myth, fable, fairy tale, religious text and picaresque prose poem, with presentiments of Surrealism and Absurdism. Lasker-Schüler herself referred to 'The Poet of Irsahab' as a grotesque, a genre then enjoying renewed interest among early modernist writers, and it is a label which could well apply to 'Ached Bey' and 'The Grand Mogul of Philippopolis' as well. In a 1998 study, Vivian Liska makes a compelling case for viewing the work as a whole as an arabesque. She denotes the characteristics of this form as 'a heterogeneous blend of diverse genres, perspectives and registers; a discontinuous temporality which runs counter to the actual, chronological passage of time, disorders time orientation and introduces a sense of time intrinsic to the work; a seemingly arbitrary structure …' – all of which holds true for *The Nights of Tino of Baghdad.*

Unlike *One Thousand and One Nights,* the great repository of Arabian storytelling with which it shares numerous motifs, *Tino* has no framing device – nor even the through line of the journey offered by *The Peter Hille Book* – and little by way of conventional exposition, with the focus often shifting abruptly between sketches. But just as its expansive geographical framework belies the book's modest dimensions, its multiplicity of forms, styles, images, references and biographical intimations make for a work of imposing scope.

The Lasker-Schüler who wrote of 'burning up in the evening colours of Jerusalem' at the outset of the 20th century is still at liberty here to fashion a Near East untouched by lived experience of the loosely defined zone then largely divided between the Ottoman, French and British empires. While her identification was complex, personal and idiosyncratic, she was following an impressive heritage in German-language letters – Lessing's *Nathan der Weise,* Goethe's *West-östlicher Divan,* Hermann von Pückler-Muskau's travel writings and the first German translations of the *Thousand and One Nights* in the mid-19th century. Karl May, better known for his enormously successful books about pioneering America, was one of the most prominent German-language writers dealing with the exotic Orient. But the literary vanguard was not immune either, with Hugo von Hofmannsthal, Peter Altenberg and Paul Scheerbart offering unconventional contributions to this vogue.

In the early 20th century, with the project of connecting Berlin to Baghdad by rail already under way, the German capital was consumed by an Oriental mania. Lasker-Schüler's reports from the circus speak of her susceptibility to colourful Orientalist motifs, and signifiers of a notional Near East were inescapable elsewhere in commercial pleasure spots and culture high and low – theatre, opera, operetta, ballet, music hall, popular song, early film, fairs, exhibitions, domestic interiors, retail environments, postcards, collectors' cards. All of them used evocative imagery for colour and exoticism, or to explore motifs that might otherwise transgress Wilhelmine mores, rather than reflecting real conditions in verifiable locations.

Similarly, when the names of familiar localities arise in *The Nights of Tino of Baghdad* – Cairo, Constantinople, Baghdad – they are not signposts to actual places so much as intertitles which invite us to enter a space in our imagination constructed from a store of received imagery. An average early 20th-century German asked to name typically 'Oriental' motifs would surely have produced a list that overlapped extensively with the book's own inventory: mosques, palaces, harems, pyramids, palm trees, sultans, slaves, eunuchs, caravans, camels – not to mention intoxicants, barbarism and sensual adventure.

Yet the book is far too singular, its dreamlike disjunction too fractured and alienating for it to serve as a colourful escapade or sensual adventure; here sex is unmistakably, almost inevitably linked to violence, transgression swiftly punished. The supposition that Lasker-Schüler had merely constructed a fictional frame through which she could momentarily abscond from the hardship and disappointments of her life, a kind of spiritual holiday home, is far too simplistic.

In choosing to adopt this realm for her own work, Else Lasker-Schüler was instead claiming ownership of something that could be, and had been, used against her – her Jewish identity. Rather than retreating further into assimilation, she strode purposefully into a world that was in part Jewish but to an even greater degree Arab. At a time of heightened antisemitism she was exploring the Semitic, embracing a highly modern idea of hybrid identity in an age of monolithic ethno-nationalism.

Parts of *Tino* read like rehearsals for new personae. In Constantinople the Princess is fitted for garments that match those of the Grand Mogul of Philippopolis, before she is cast out from the court to end up as a donkey driver, again dressed as a man. Tino cross-dresses to witness executions alongside her uncle in 'Ached Bey', which captures Lasker-Schüler in what Vivian Liska calls an 'emancipatory moment', one particularly associated with her role as a poet, with the flow of the young foreigner's blood signalling the start of an artistic odyssey.

In Tino's world these ritualistic acts of violence are offered in the same scriptural, mythic style as the raptures of sensual love. Beguiling portmanteaux – *rauschesüß, Nebelweinen* – often blur the categories of qualifying and qualified, joining contrivances like the Khedive fish and the forest of Pharaoh trees (which recur in one of the author's most famous verses, 'Heimweh',

1917). As well as the wilful punctuation, one arresting element is the recurrence of clipped, untranslated, 'foreign' text. The contemporary reader may well have imagined these words to be Arabic. In fact they issued from a fantasy language of Lasker-Schüler's devising which she variously termed 'Syrian' or 'Asiatic'; at one point she was arrested in Prague for giving an impromptu al fresco address in her invented tongue for an audience which included Franz Kafka.

Tino reflects Lasker-Schüler's growing confidence as she seeks inspiration further from her own life. It contains fewer encrypted figures than *Hille* yet it is impossible not to draw inferences about some characters. Ached Bey, for instance, may represent her first husband Berthold Lasker, but is also thought to be based on Lasker-Schüler's own uncle Leopold Sonnemann, a highly prominent banker and publisher who disapproved of his bohemian niece. 'Pull' (Paul) returns, and behind the mask of the kindly Plumm Pasha who accepts the protagonist's child as his own we may well see adoptive father Herwarth Walden; that he lavishes gifts on the child may represent wish fulfilment on the part of his struggling mother. The treacherous brothers of 'The Poet of Irsahab' are thought to be modelled on two of the author's own siblings, less favoured than her beloved Paul.

If we pursue these biographical inferences further, two characters in particular stand out. The five short pieces of the 'Apollydes' cycle concern Tino's love for a handsome Greek boy who has consecrated his life to love. The first, 'Tino to Apollydes', is 52 words long and mentions the '52 moons' during which Tino was veiled, thought to be a reference to the duration of the author's marriage to Berthold Lasker before their separation. She later claimed that Paul's father was a Greek man she had met in the street; in a 1917 letter to Karl Kraus she calls him Alcibiades de Rouan, a name so fanciful it hardly functions as deflection. But might Apollydes be a stand-in for this stranger?

The identity of Senna Pasha is no secret: Senna Hoy, also the dedicatee of the 1919 edition (the first edition being dedicated to the author's mother). Senna Hoy's idiosyncratic 1904 novella *Goldene Kätie* references both Lasker-Schüler and Tino, and he later wrote of his love for 'the Judaic maiden Tino'. At the time Lasker-Schüler was writing he was in the Russian Empire eagerly following the revolutionary upheavals there, having fled harassment by the Prussian authorities. What to make of Tino's urging: 'By the Great Prophet, Senna Pasha, keep my secret in your heart'? What secret is this? In a biography of Lasker-Schüler, Kerstin Decker suggests that Senna Hoy was in fact the father of Lasker-Schüler's son, and certainly he bore a resemblance to Paul. This would have been a highly illicit encounter; not only was Lasker-Schüler married but Johannes, as he was then, was a minor. And drawing these two lines of enquiry together – in a 1910 letter Lasker-Schüler referred to Senna Hoy as 'Alcibiades'. Senna Hoy was imprisoned by the Russian authorities just as *Tino* was published. This lends an edge of prophecy to the book's recurring motif of handsome young men – Apollydes, Minn, the unnamed Jew executed by Ached Bey – suffering at the hands of tyrannical patriarchs.

The Walden-Lasker-Schüler blended family trio was by now a familiar sight in Berlin's literary hub, the Café des Westens ('the little family lived, I suspect, on nothing but coffee,' sniffed actor Tilla Durieux). But Else Lasker-Schüler was not just an eccentric bohemian, she was an important figure at the forefront of an emergent, as-yet unnamed movement, identifying profoundly with the avant-garde and serving with valour in the culture wars of Wilhelmine Germany. In this prolific period she wrote her first drama, *Die Wupper*, named for the river that ran through her home town, and in 1910 the first of her many contributions to one of the most significant journals of early modernism, for which she also supplied the name: *Der Sturm*.

Published by Walden, *Der Sturm* became a house organ for the movement soon badged as 'Expressionism' (the record is undecided if it was Walden or Kurt Hiller who supplied the name). But it also became a window onto the stormy relations between Lasker-Schüler and her husband, who had embarked on an affair. Lasker-Schüler chronicled their split in deceptively blithe dispatches with a wealth of gossipy bohemian detail under the rubric 'Letters to Norway' (Walden was on a Nordic journey at the time). It is to Walden's credit that he ran this public unravelling of his marriage in *Der Sturm*, which Lasker-Schüler issued for a wider readership in 1912 as the book *Mein Herz* (My Heart).

These letters also introduced a new persona forged from the failure of her second (and last) marriage: 'In the night of my greatest misery I promoted myself to Prince of Thebes' – an invented entity which

Lasker-Schüler fused with the biblical Joseph. It is telling that in her distress she should return to a figure with such rich childhood associations, one that bound her not just to memories of her beloved brother and mother, but also her early socialisation. She would recount the story of Joseph and his brothers in school; on one occasion a fellow pupil interjected to declare – prophetically – that Else *was* Joseph.

And now indeed she was, taking her place in the lineage of artists who draw no distinction between invention and existence. Her creativity was a continuum of verse, prose, drama, art, performance, costume, correspondence and everyday life, her ideas manifested not just in what she published or exhibited but also in how she presented herself to her fellow human beings. Lover Gottfried Benn reported that 'you couldn't cross the street without everyone stopping and watching her: extravagant, broad skirts or trousers, ridiculous upper garments, neck and arms draped in flashy costume jewellery.' She now often signed letters as Jussuf and/or the Prince of Thebes.

In 1913 Lasker-Schüler developed a treatment for a moving picture entitled 'Plumm-Pascha', featuring Tino, Diwagâtme, Hassan and the titular character. It was part of *Das Kinobuch* (The Cinema Book), a visionary undertaking for which Leipzig theatre critic Kurt Pinthus enlisted his Expressionist writer friends; other contributors included Max Brod, Albert Ehrenstein and Elsa Asenijeff. The project embraced cinema at a critical moment in its development. Films still hadn't entirely shaken their novelty status, but the writers believed that given sufficient scope, the new form might properly aspire to the status accorded to novels or paintings. None of their treatments were ever developed, but considering that Expressionism would be a key mode of Germany's explosion of cinematic brilliance after World War One, *Das Kinobuch* can be seen as something of a game plan, a vision of filmic excellence projected into the future.

Lasker-Schüler's contribution shares motifs with the chapter of the same name in *The Nights of Tino of Baghdad,* but it is a stand-alone scenario which collapses dynastic and Ottoman Egypt into a single plane and adds elements of *A Midsummer Night's Dream*. It represents a fascinating stylistic transformation; the narrative is just as absurd as the *Tino* tales, the characters no less singular, but the format renders their exploits in a clipped, utilitarian style – a bracing distillate of the heady, evocative prose of *Tino:*

> The Grand Vizier is lying on the roof, roaring; suddenly a balloon appears with 'Occident' written on it. Dr Eisenbart climbs out of the balloon onto the roof, followed by living bottles with the inscription 'Cow Lymph'. The servants want to prevent the inquisitive doctor from examining the angry Pasha. But they do not manage to prevent Dr Eisenbart from extracting lymph from the bull, until the Grand Vizier bites off its head; it is impaled on a long pole as a warning. Meanwhile the wise men approach and relay Diwagâtme's wise words. The Vizier utters a roar of joy, stumbles a few times over the carpet on his roof and the wise men with him.

In 1913 Lasker-Schüler also issued a book of essays as well as *Hebräische Balladen* (Hebrew Ballads), a volume of poetry which represented an even deeper engagement with her Jewish roots, with most of its verses named for figures from the Torah. That year, at a time when she could barely keep herself in coffee, she somehow gathered the funds to visit Senna Hoy in Moscow where he had been imprisoned in an asylum, and desperately tried to gain attention for his plight. But he died the following year, aged just 31 – a terrible blow for Lasker-Schüler. He was buried in the Weißensee Jewish cemetery in Berlin.

Der Prinz von Theben (The Prince of Thebes) appeared in the summer of 1914, issued by Leipzig publisher Verlag der weißen Bücher. However, most of its constituent texts had appeared previously in *Der Sturm* and other venues, dating as far back as 1908. This places the book in a line of direct creative succession to *Tino,* despite the seven years between them. It is as long as *Hille,* yet it contains just eleven stories (or nine if you count the 'Abigail' cycle as one unit). Its geographic scope is even greater, extending as far afield as India and Afghanistan, while its temporal coordinates are biblical, medieval, colonial and timelessly Oriental – a thousand and one nights and the five books of Moses.

While no less elliptical than the other two books here, *The Prince of Thebes* allows its stories to evolve rather than smash-cutting between scenes. Their discrete development makes them less porous, more self-contained, and with remarkably little dialogue they have a notable depth and roundedness. It is probably no coincidence that – as far as we can make out – Lasker-Schüler largely eschewed biographical ciphers. One exception is 'Marc ben Ruben of Cana', a reference to her artist friend Franz Marc, who supplied three colour images to the edition to complement the author's own monochrome illustrations. Here her loyalties are generally signalled by dedications, including Marc again and the book's publisher Erik-Ernst Schwabach, while figures like Conradin and Chandragupta are selected for suggestive resonance rather than historical accuracy. The three men named Abigail (a name otherwise only ever applied to women) form an internal rhyme with the three Chandraguptas, like the recurring Ismael-Hamed and the figure of Schlôme/Schalôme. The 'Princess from Baghdad' is mentioned or implied in 'The Sheik', 'The Dervish', 'The Fakir' and 'The Crusade', and armed with our back knowledge we can identify her as Tino. Lilâme and Diwagâtme also reappear, although it isn't apparent if these figures are co-extensive or coincidental, unlike the Fakir who appears unchanged since his unsettling debut.

Like the absurdist trip to contemporary Berlin in *Tino,* and the recollection of parting from Petrus in 1903 which snaps us out of a land beyond (once upon a) time in *Hille,* Lasker-Schüler once again evokes timelessness only to spike it with specificity. Here it is in 'The Dervish' where we find 'English ladies', images of fragile Edwardian gentility on an Egyptian expedition, garnishing a bloodbath with gothic blossoms. But there is also a cyclical momentum, with lullabies, suggestions of

Nietzsche (the 'dancing star' from *Also sprach Zarathustra*) and hints of the Germanic forest taking us back to *Hille;* the Christian sisters could be Sage and Haidekraut grown up.

The eroticism and violence bubbling underground in *Hille,* which then poured forth from *Tino,* here burst their banks entirely and merge as they flow. The book is submerged in the carnal: homoeroticism, cannibalism, sado-masochism, transvestism and – depending how we interpret the fate of Singa in the temple built on her dead son's bones – incestuous necrophilia. The barbarism assumes monstrous proportions in the fantastically bloody Shiite rites of 'The Dervish', the oedipal savagery which bookends the Abigail cycle and the brutal vengeance of the spurned Chandragupta in a section simply entitled 'Der Amokläufer' (The Maniac) in the first edition. The figures in *The Prince of Thebes* are insistently drawn to their origins – to humanity's base animalistic state, to the earth, to the womb, to childhood, or to Creation; the serpentine Fakir brings erotic disgrace like Eden's original emissary of sin. While Lasker-Schüler was never the most avid chronicler of her time, it is striking that in 'The Crusader' her book ends with a great clash of civilisations just as Europe was descending into the Great War.

Here and in the first text we also find one of the most persistent themes in the work of Else Lasker-Schüler – the reconciliation of faiths (in this case through the common enemy of another religion). Lasker-Schüler's images for the book depicted a romanticised Near East where crescent moons nestle harmoniously with six-pointed stars, recalling Petrus and Tino visiting each other's places of worship in *Hille* and *Tino*'s Caliph remembering 'the Jewess of his youth'. It is no accident that Lasker-Schüler should choose Joseph/Yosef/Yusuf, common to all three Abrahamic religions, as a point of identification. In 1909 she wrote to Karl Kraus: 'In Baghdad a sorceress once told me that I had lain many thousands of years as a mummy in a vault and that I was no more or no less than Joseph, which is Jussuf in Arabic' (corresponding with Else Lasker-Schüler required an unusual degree of imagination and forbearance).

But in contrast to her letters of the time, Lasker-Schüler does not speak through Yusuf/the Prince here, and his entrance in the book named for him is conspicuously inconspicuous. After mention of his famous cloak in 'The Dervish', where the figures of Tino and Yusuf merge through the donning of a garment – fashion is never trivial in Lasker-Schüler's prose – he then shuffles, unnamed, into the reader's awareness in the account of Abigail II. Soon, however, he is elevated from court painter to Melech through ambition and charisma (not to mention regicide) to become the third Abigail. Lasker-Schüler signed a number of her letters to Franz Marc as Abigail, and it is a striking insight into her priorities that two of the rulers of that name should be a poet and an artist; even the micro-managing tyrant Abigail II is a scholar.

Striking too is that the two favoured Abigails should be handsome youths; throughout her life Lasker-Schüler was persistently and openly attracted to younger men. The second and third Abigails share her tastes; we witness a reverse exoticism by which Yusuf yearns for blond warriors like an Occidental adventurer lusting after Levantine odalisques. But desire compromises his martial project, whereas Tino overcomes her attraction to kill the thing she loves and fulfil her mission. It is not difficult to imagine the two as warring elements of Lasker-Schüler's own complex character.

The Prince of Thebes is largely free of neologisms, but Lasker-Schüler's private language returns. One could arguably place these lines alongside phonetic experiments practised by her fellow Expressionists, or by the Futurists and Dadaists; witness Hugo Ball's later verse 'Karawane'. It may also be that their impenetrable otherness stood for a part of the author's identity that would remain indecipherable. It functioned like the flute with which she posed for a photograph yet could not play (an image actually produced for a projected stage presentation, *Der Fakir von Theben,* which was never realised).

In *The Prince of Thebes* we have an insight into Lasker-Schüler's strategies, not just as a writer but as an individual making her way in the world. The book emerged from a particularly challenging phase of her life, but Lasker-Schüler rarely responded to hardship with despondency, irony or self-deprecation; remember, this is the woman who penned her own bible. Instead, in the words of Judith Kuckart we witness a 'militant ecstasy which is awakened when the writer bangs her head against reality'.

In an exhaustive 2020 study, Johanna Meixner traces the androgyny of Lasker-Schüler's avatars throughout her prose, noting that 'each disguise is made transparent as such to the reader, i.e. from it a form of androgyny is constituted which certainly does not consist of a harmonious combination of male and female coded properties or features – the androgynous poetic ideal of Romanticism – but rather shows the performative aspect of gender and the culturally determined demarcation between genders.' The variously named – at times nameless – protagonist falls through time, place, ethnicity, gender and sexuality, a kind of Orientalist Orlando. In fact the inspiration for *Orlando,* Vita Sackville-West, met Lasker-Schüler in Berlin in 1928 and wrote to the book's author, lover Virginia Woolf, that she was 'not unworthy to be a denizen of Virginia's world.'

Lasker-Schüler's engagement with the 'Orient' was clearly not a fact-finding mission but nor was it a mere flirtation with exotica; instead it represented immersion through identification. The minds of many present-day readers will naturally turn to post-colonial theory, particularly Edward Said's landmark 1978 study *Orientalism.* But it is also worth noting that 'Orientals' was an offensive term applied to Jews in Lasker-Schüler's time, and that adopting it for herself was an act of positive reclamation comparable to shifting use of the word 'queer'. The 'wild Jew' who recurs in Lasker-Schüler's prose – belligerent, ungovernable, free – represents the antithesis of assimilation, the Jew who has endured a 'life of degradation' in the words of Martin Buber, yet 'remained Oriental throughout it all'.

Lasker-Schüler's alertness and sympathy to difference seems to abandon her in the face of 'black' and 'Negro' characters (it is not apparent where she draws the distinction). Almost always appearing as servants, they are rarely trusted with the agency of even the lowliest Arab. In an essay about her one-time art teacher Simson Goldberg, Lasker-Schüler mentioned that she went with him to a 'Völkerschau' in late 19th-century Berlin, where inhabitants of Germany's African colonies were presented like zoo animals, and even many years later she offers no condemnation of this abject spectacle, no judgement at all other than: 'exotic'.

Else Lasker-Schüler never designated the three books presented here as a triptych, but it is impossible to ignore their links and similarities. In fact they are difficult to compare with anything of their time *except* each other. They are all short, fragmentary works made up of epics masquerading as miniatures, and if their digressive density is at times alienating it is because they are tracing the development of a sensibility rather than a grand narrative in the 19th-century sense. Their prose is anything but prosaic, crafted with a rapacious appetite for words entirely piqued by poetry. They all issued from a concentrated burst of creative energy, their production largely confined to the period 1905 to 1910. They share numerous characters and motifs while tracing the arc of a remarkable transformation. We first find Tino in *The Peter Hille Book,* timid, lost, a blank slate of identity crouching beneath the rock and the might of Petrus. In *The Nights of Tino of Baghdad* she ventures out into a bright and hazardous world and encounters the raptures of love, yet she is still beholden to patriarchal power. Finally, in *The Prince of Thebes* we witness her apotheosis as a triumphant warrior princess, burning bright in the evening colours of Jerusalem.

Directly after the publication of *The Prince of Thebes* the outbreak of World War One found Lasker-Schüler in Munich. She was still dressing in character as 'a dream from the Orient' in the words of writer Emmy Hennings who witnessed her at the time. But in a misguided attempt at patriotic appeasement she also draped herself with flags and medals. In an atmosphere of heightened sensitivities she was arrested no less than four times within a matter of weeks.

The end of the war and the demise of the Wilhelmine order offered Lasker-Schüler a more sympathetic environment for her creative undertakings and everyday eccentricities, and she entered the Weimar Republic on something of an artistic high. She witnessed the first staging of her major dramatic work *Die Wupper* and gave numerous presentations of her writing throughout Europe, including an appearance at the Bauhaus in its early, heterodox phase. She also gained greater exposure for her graphic works which were not just seen in exhibitions but also on the covers of a ten-volume edition of her writing issued by gallerist Paul Cassirer which included a new title, a roman à clef entitled *Der Malik* which picked up on the 'Abigail' cycle from *The Prince of Thebes*.

But success was relative for Lasker-Schüler, and rarely paired with financial reward. For this she blamed her publishers, and in 1925 she took aim at Cassirer, Juncker and the rest of them in a bitter pamphlet. She could be a splenetic adversary, holding strong opinions of her contemporaries, and vice versa – Gottfried Benn adored her, Franz Kafka couldn't stand her. But she was also intensely loyal, dedicating works to favoured associates or honouring them in pen sketches, and she was consistently generous to those (even) less fortunate than herself.

Lasker-Schüler's son Paul, who had shown great promise as an artist, was now gravely ill with tuberculosis. All of his mother's limited funds were now going on his treatment and she moved into the Berlin studio of Palestinian Jewish artist Jussuf Abbo to tend to him. To no avail; Paul Lasker-Schüler died in 1927 and was laid to rest in the Jewish cemetery at Weißensee – just a few metres from Senna Hoy. His mother never truly recovered, but her own darkness was soon engulfed by the worsening conditions in late Weimar Germany; in 1930 she was assaulted by Nazi thugs at the Berlin premiere of the film *All Quiet on the Western Front.*

In 1932 Lasker-Schüler at least found belated recognition from the literary establishment when she was awarded the prestigious Kleist Prize, for which she had long petitioned. But it was of little use once the Nazis came to power, barely two months later. As an independent woman disinclined to keep her views to herself, as a representative of modernist literature, as a known supporter of homosexuals and anarchists, and of course as a Jew – a Jew who drew attention to her identity, no less – there was clearly no place for Else Lasker-Schüler in the Third Reich.

She left Berlin in April 1933, never to return, and settled in circumstances of the utmost precarity in Zurich, where authorities barely tolerated her presence. She solicited aid from Thomas Mann in the guise of the

Prince of Thebes and extended a greeting to his wife Katia, 'the Caliph's daughter'; Lasker-Schüler may well have been reminding Mann that his Jewish wife might have shared her fate.

In 1934 Else Lasker-Schüler had her first encounter with the real-life counterpart of a realm in which so much of her writing was located, yet the first reports of her trip to Palestine were still dominated by ideals rather than observations. She returned in 1937 and again in 1939, but as World War Two broke out Swiss authorities denied her re-entry. Poor and isolated, she settled in Jerusalem but still remembered those (even) less fortunate than herself, joining protests when British Mandate authorities stemmed the flow of Jewish refugees from Europe. Nor was she blind to tensions between Jews and Arabs ('our brothers at heart') in her adoptive home. Her proposal for ensuring harmony may have been whimsical, even provocatively so – it essentially amounted to sending everyone to a funfair – but underlying it was the far-sighted knowledge that segregating a multi-ethnic nation would bring suffering.

Else Lasker-Schüler's last book, *Mein blaues Klavier* (My Blue Piano), appeared in 1943; its verses find her aching for her homeland, her culture, her language, the house where she grew up. That year the house was destroyed in a bombing raid. Else Lasker-Schüler died in January 1945 and was buried on the Mount of Olives, her prophecy of burning up in the evening colours of Jerusalem fulfilled.

Else Lasker-Schüler's homecoming took longer than her present unassailable status as one of the most important German modernists might suggest. Even in the late 1960s, when author Heinrich Böll proposed a memorial to mark the 100th anniversary of her birth, he found little interest. The mid-1970s brought reissues and new productions of her major dramatic work, *Die Wupper,* while the writer even appeared on a West German stamp. This revival was largely focused on her verse, which was absorbed into the canon, extensively anthologised, set as standard texts in German schools and translated into English in a number of different editions. Meanwhile the prose titles to which Else Lasker-Schüler devoted a significant proportion of her career were long regarded as secondary, particularly the earliest examples, which were ascribed 'merely historical or biographical interest', dismissed as 'not really enjoyable' or even 'unreadable'. It is only in the last two decades or so that these works have been subject to earnest critical reappraisal and recognised as the profound, rich, multi-faceted works that they are, an essential and indivisible part of one of the greatest literary careers of the 20th century.